A STRANGER TO HIMSELF

WILLIAM POST

authorHOUSE®

AuthorHouse™
1663 Liberty Drive
Bloomington, IN 47403
www.authorhouse.com
Phone: 1 (800) 839-8640

Published by AuthorHouse   08/03/2017

ISBN: 978-1-5462-0260-8 (sc)
ISBN: 978-1-5462-0307-0 (e)

OTHER BOOKS BY WILLIAM POST

The Mystery of Table Mountain

The Miracle

A Call to Duty

Gold Fever

The Blue Ridge

A Doctor by War

Inner Circles

The Evolution of Nora

Darlene

The Tides of War

The First Crossing of America

Some Boys From Texas

Alaskan Paranormal

The Grey Fox

Captain My Captain

The Law and Alan Taylor

The Riflemen

A Soldier and A Sailor

A New Eden

Lost in Indian Country

A Trip to California

Kelly Andrews

Lost in the Ukraine

A Ghost Tribe

A Change in Tradition

A Stranger to Himself

Pure Love

A Promise to a Friend

Sid Porter

A Gathering of a Family

Hard Times

Wrong Place - Wrong Time

CONTENTS

PREFACE

This story takes a boy through to manhood and beyond about ten years. The war turns the boy into a vicious fighting man. He feels himself changing and cannot stop it and stay alive. Four years of the war makes him a hard man. The war had turned him against all humanity, and he just wants to be alone and away from everyone and the war.

As this story goes from through the Civil War and after, it is in the Cowboy Era. That era only lasted about fifty years, yet it is probably the most indelible period in America according to many. The lawless West and the men who braved it, formed the Cowboy Era. Many hardened men from the war invaded the West in search of a new life.

Going west, Thomas Benson never asked for trouble, but was more than prepared to meet it when it happened. He finds himself wondering who he is. He was a tender, caring boy when he was pushed into the war at age twenty, but comes out a hardened, vicious fighter four years later.

Thomas Benson has never known a woman's love, other than his mothers, as the War gave no time or place for that. It is hard for him to love, but slowly he returns to a caring person again, intermingled with some tough situations which happened in the old West.

CHAPTER 1

BOY TO MAN

Thomas was born in New York City to Keith and Matti Benson. Keith was a descendant of the Rothschild family, and had been groomed in England before being sent to America to a bank they owned. He was now president of the largest bank in the city.

He met his wife, Matti, at a social function in England, and after a year's courtships, she became his wife. She was a devoted mother. She was educated, and had gone through three years of an English finishing school. She was quiet, and Thomas took on her personality.

Thomas was a precocious child, so with a devoted mother, he progressed in academics quickly. As the public schools were too slow for Thomas, his mother taught him through the first four grades.

Matti was athletic. Her family prided themselves in running, and had some notoriety doing so. She ran with Thomas everyday, excepting bad weather. Thomas loved to run with his mother. She was five-nine, and had a slim body. She could always out do Thomas. She passed onto Thomas the joy of running.

Keith had heard of a private teacher who took on eight students a year. He was expensive, but his friends assured him that he was worth it. Thomas attended two years under this man. He was strict and required much from his students. Even though Thomas was bright, the length of the homework required three hours nearly every night.

The other students were children of Keith's colleagues. All were now being sent to boarding school in Andover. Matti did not want Thomas going there. She had heard many stories about boys who went there. She didn't know if they were true, but she would not take the chance.

Thomas' teacher left New York the next year. Matti had heard of a woman teacher named Sandra Stone. She was said to be the best, so she enrolled Thomas. Sandra had only four students. To Thomas' surprise, the others students were girls. They were all extremely bright. Although Thomas was not smarter than the three, he vowed to outwork them. Most of the time, hard work will trump acumen.

Miss Stone was twenty-six and was a college graduate. She also was very bright. Her personality was bubbly, and the students really liked her. Instead of being strict like his last teacher, Miss Stone seemed part of the group, and laughed and had fun while she taught. This made all want to study hard to please her.

She liked to show experiments, and often had an interesting experiment to express the science lesson of the day.

The room where they were taught had a cloakroom just behind the classroom to hang their coats and store backpacks. It was open on both ends, but was only six feet wide. At lunch they always went to a deli that was close by.

One day as they went to get their coats, Carol Lombard caught Thomas alone in the cloakroom and said, Thomas, I want to have an experiment with you. Thomas was somewhat shocked and said, "What is the experiment, Carol?"

"I have never kissed a boy. I want you to kiss me, so we can both know what it's like."

Thomas was reluctant to do this, but always wanted to please people, so he puckers up with his eyes closed. Carol came to him, and put her lips on his, closed lips of course. Just as they made contact, Miss Stone came into the cloakroom and said, "What are you two doing?"

Carol stood back and said, "We were just conducting an experiment, Miss Stone. You see, neither of us have ever had a kiss, and we were wondering what it was like."

Thomas was thinking, *"Where did she get the 'we' part of this."*

Miss Stone said, "Very good, Carol, but experiments should be shown to the entire class. After lunch, I expect you to share your experiment with the class."

In the deli, Thomas and Carol took a table where just the two sat. Carol said, "Let's surprise Miss Stone. When she asks us to get up, we will be about six feet apart. You will say, 'Carol, my darling,' then we will run to each others arms, and you will bend me over in a mad kiss. When we pull apart, go to your knees and say, 'After that kiss, I must ask for your

3

hand in marriage.' I will turn to the class and hold my heart with both hands and say, 'you have stolen my heart, Thomas.' We will use dramatic voices."

Thomas grinned and said, "You're the greatest, Carol, I'll do it."

After lunch Miss Stone told them to come forward. They went through their routine, and it came off marvelously. The two other girls and Miss Stone clapped. She said, "No matter how I try, you children out do me every time. I enjoyed your kiss like I was part of it. Please don't tell your parents about this, or they may kick me out."

Although he saw Miss Stone's point, Thomas couldn't wait to tell his mother. She laughed so hard, she held her sides. She said, "I know Carol, but she always seems so quiet and reserve."

"She's anything but that mother. She's spontaneous and a riot. She keeps the class laughing most of the times. But as good as she is, she's not even in it with Miss Stone. I would like to marry Miss Stone when I'm grown."

"She'll be an old woman by then, Thomas."

"Miss Stone will never be an old woman, mother. I'll bet she stays young and happy for the next fifty years."

Matti said, "Well, if you gave Carol a kiss, you must give your mother two kisses."

Thomas kissed her and said, "No one will ever take your place, Mother," and they hugged.

By the time Thomas was fifteen, he was ready for college. His mother wanted him to become a doctor. Not having a propensity toward any vocation, Thomas acquiesced to her wishes, and studied pre-med.

Thomas did his best with his studies. He was always first in his class. He also ran on the schools track team and was excellent there, also.

Thomas loved learning new things. He read avidly with his mother structuring this activity, as she was an avid reader, also. When Thomas was eighteen, he applied and was accepted into Mt. Sinai School of Medicine. His mother had filled out his application, and put down that he was twenty-one. She did this in fear they would not take a boy so young in age.

He found that most of the students were on an even par with him academically, but none worked as hard as Thomas, so he was near if not first in every subject.

He had a great relationships with his professors. He asked interesting questions that were pertinent and challenging. They all liked him and particularly the head of the medical school, Dr. Edwin Phillips. They had many long conversations, mostly about medicine. Dr. Phillips could see Thomas was going to be a master at medicine. Doctor Bernstein often joined their conversations.

Dr. Bernstein said, "Thomas has the most skilled hands I have ever seen at this medical school. Just watch how he ties sutures. His hands work so fast you can barely see them. And he makes incisions with such precision, he looks like a skilled surgeon of many years. His kind only comes along once in a lifetime, Ed."

Thomas was never around women, that distraction never bothered him because he was kept busy, except when he ran with his mother.

In the middle of his third year in medical school, Ft. Sumner was fired upon. Nearly all the seniors were given their medical licenses early, and went to war. Thomas didn't, because his mother forbade it. Also Dr. Phillips encouraged him to finish medical school.

Thomas invited Dr. Phillips, Dr. Bernstein and their wives to dinner often, so his parents knew them quite well. The Bensons lived in a large house that had a dining room that would seat about twenty people. They also employed several servants. Next door lived the vise president of the bank, Barney Dowd. He was a shirttail relative that Keith particularly liked. They were actually like bothers. He and his wife, Betty, were also present at these dinners.

CHAPTER 2

THE WAR

Just two months before he was to graduate, Thomas was conscripted into the army. Although they tried, Thomas could not be exempted. Because of their attempt to keep Thomas out, he was put into the infantry. Being a college graduate, he was commissioned.

The captain of his company was Colin Smith, who had a reputation of uncommon valor. He was a West Point graduate and was heralded as a superb leader. Thomas admired him as did everyone. Colin not only had a voice that resonated, but looked the part better than anyone he had ever seen.

The battle of Manassas had already been fought when Thomas arrived, but another battle was on the brink of happening when he joined his company in Maryland. The battle of South Mountain occurred, and it was a Union Victory. Everyone was in high spirits. Thomas' company had been held back, and was only in on the mopping up, as the Rebels were routed.

The next battle his company was thrust into the heart of the battle. Thomas lead a squad. His squad performed admirably as they had a sergeant who inspired the men, most of which died in battle. Thomas was so scared he could barely function. He put one foot in front of the other, and just keep moving. Bullets were flying. A man on each side of him was hit, but he just kept moving, and yelling at the top of his lungs. He found that yelling really helped to suppress the fear that overwhelmed him.

Although Thomas did nothing heroic, his captain noted the unit was his best, and pinned a metal on Thomas. The colonel said before the troops, "This man is the inspiration of our company. Follow this man!"

Thomas thought, *"Sergeant Brown was the inspiration, but he's dead, and I'm taking his glory."* However, he knew better than to express this. His company, led by Colin, performed marvelously. He had been given another sergeant who was nearly as good as Brown. Thomas talked to him and said, "Sergeant Purvis, most of these troops are raw recruits. We must inspire them. Captain Smith puts us in strategic positions to be successful, let's not let him down. Keep talking to the men, and I will do my best to lead them. I've only been here a short time, but I have learned a lot. Success is nearly always followed by our inspiring the men."

"Purvis said, "I'll do my best, Lieutenant," and he did. The next battle was severe, and they lost nearly half their men, although Thomas did his best to put them in less vulnerable positions.

Captain Smith noticed and said, "Lieutenant, you are a born leader. Keep up the good work." Purvis was by him when Smith made the remark, and thought how lucky he was to be with a seasoned leader like Lieutenant Benson.

Thomas thought, "If he had any idea of how scared I am, he would send me to the rear."

Their next engagement was no different than the previous battle. Bullets were teeming, and many men died who were as close as two feet from him. Purvis was wounded badly and Thomas found him and carried him on his shoulders to the rear and laid him down.

Purvis said, "I can't tell you what a privilege it was to serve under you."

A major was near and heard Purvis, and was greatly impressed. He asked Purvis who Thomas was after he had left. Purvis said, "That's Lieutenant Benson, Sir, the best fighting man I have ever fought with."

Thomas left and rejoined his outfit. The battle had subsided as both armies withdrew. There were lulls between battles and Thomas spent that time getting replacements and having the veterans of his squad talk to the new recruits. Thomas didn't even shave yet, but right from the start he smeared grease on his cheeks and chin and then used soot to put on the grease. It made him look like he had a beard. This made him look much older. It gave him a hard look.

Thomas could see himself changing each week. He was no longer a boy from college, but a killer. Every battle he personally killed men. He carried a repeating rifle that he could work the lever with great speed. He had confiscated the weapon from a dead soldier. It used the same caliber bullets as the issued rifles, but held twenty-eight cartridges he could fire at one time without reloading.

He now counted himself dead as he had seen so many fall that he knew it was just a matter of time for a bullet to take him. After he did that, he saw he had little fear. If you were dead already, what was there to fear?

Battle after battle Thomas fought with his men. They died all around him, but he was never wounded.

Thomas could tell he had really changed. He went from a mild and quiet person to a vicious warrior who yelled throughout the battle. This inspired his men to shout and fight viciously. He never wanted to count the men he killed, but in spite of himself he kept count. The number was twenty-two when he became the company commander through attrition. Colin Smith and been kicked up to battalion commander.

They were now at Harper's Ferry. They were routed there, and only by a stoke of luck did Thomas live through that battle. He was running, leading his company, when he tripped and fell into a crater. Just ahead where he would have been, a cannon ball hit and exploded. Many of his men were killed there. After the battle, when the smoke cleared, half his company was gone.

He had no friends, he just knew their names. Even his fellow officers had little to do with him as he kept to himself, and was known for his killing ability. Not mixing with anyone was on purpose. When he sent men out, they were usually killed, and he didn't want to know them. He happened to hear a sergeant telling another soldier. "You don't want to be around Benson until the bullets start flying, then you want to be as close to him as possible."

Thomas' company was relieved to regroup. Replacements were raw and he knew he must put them with seasoned veterans. He talked to his new sergeant. He was a big man, and looked tough.

He said, "Sergeant, Scatter these recruits with the veterans. They may freeze, but with a veteran next to them, they won't, because the veterans won't let them."

When they returned to the line, the battle of Shepardstow was on. They had the superior numbers, but Lee out flanked them, and they were routed again. Most felt they could have won that day, but McClellan chose to retreat. The only thing that saved them was Lee had run so low on supplies, that he could not chase them.

Lincoln was so mad at McClellan for withdrawing, when he had ten-thousand more troops than Lee, that he removed him from command. McClellan was furious, but could do nothing.

There was a pause while Lee replaced his supplies and Lincoln found another general. This general did not fit exactly what Lincoln wanted, so he chose another. He finally settled on U. S. Grant.

What Lincoln saw in Grant was a winner. Grant pressed the enemy, even when it looked badly to do so. Grant went around fourteen generals senior to him, which made him unpopular. However, he had two great friends in Bill Sheridan and Phil Sherman. The three met with Lincoln, and he told them that there could be no let up.

McClellan had been nominated by the Democrats to run

against Lincoln in the coming presidential race to take place in November of 1863.

Lincoln said, "If I don't get a decisive victory before the election, McClellan will win and sue for peace. It will divide our nation and slavery will continue. We must win at all costs."

Grant said, "It will cost many more lives with that strategy, Mr. President, but it may be the only way to win. I'll do what you say, as keeping the Union together must be done."

The last battle before the pause was a hard fought battle. It was during this battle that Thomas' company was again at the point of attack. His company was put there on purpose. Thomas was at the head of the spearhead. He had run about two hundred steps when his first sergeant grabbed his ankle, and he fell into a shell hole with Sergeant Rimes beside him.

Thomas yelled, "What did you do that for, Sergeant?"

"Because we can't let you be killed. You're the leader of company, and we would be lost without you. You don't have to lead in every battle, Sir."

Eighty percent of the company died that day, but it was a resounding victory.

Right after that battle, Thomas was transferred to a cavalry unit. Somehow his record got mixed up with another Thomas Benson's record. The other Benson was an outstanding cavalry officer, but had been killed.

Thomas knew how to ride, but was not particularly good at it. He knew he had to get good in a hurry. He took rides with a sergeant and said, "We need to know this area like the back of hands. It may save our lives. They rode everyday very hard.

It took Thomas awhile to catch up to the ability of the others, but he did. One of the men said, "I heard Captain Benson was wounded badly, and can't quite keep up now, but you just wait, when he goes into battle stay close to him, and you may live."

Thomas rode into his first battle next to two men who were the best warriors he ever saw. They kept their saber in their strong hand, and their pistol in the other, their rein was put over the saddle horn and they used their spurs to urge their steeds on, and their knees to give their horses direction. He tried to emulate their fighting, and after awhile, became quite good. He always had his lever action repeater. Once his pistol was empty, he sheathed his sword and began using the repeater. He was deadly with it. He began to add to the number of men he killed and he was now past forty.

One of the soldiers said, "I've never seen a man as quick as Captain Benson. Just watch his hands working the lever of his rifle when he's fighting."

The soldier he was talking to said, "You watch his hands, I'm just trying to stay alive."

Thomas had grown to be six-two that matched his fathers height. The constant activity had given him great physical strength. He wore a short beard and mustache, now, and didn't need the grease and soot. He had sharp features to start with, and the hair on his face made him look hard, as he never smiled.

A Lieutenant Howard Estep was assigned to him. Howard was not new to the war. His company had suffered so many casualties, they disbanded the company and sent Howard to Thomas.

Thomas interviewed him. He asked, "How long have you been in combat, Lieutenant?"

A little over a year, Sir. I'm surprised I have lived this long."

"We all feel that way, Lieutenant. Stay close to me tomorrow, I will need you."

And indeed he did. When fighting, Thomas was surrounded, but Howard came to his aid, and together they fought off the three men, killing all three."

"You're a good soldier, Lieutenant. I thought this was my day when those three had me, but just then there you were, and rescued me."

"I don't know who rescued whom, Captain. Without you, I would now be in the arms of Jesus."

"That's a comforting thought, Lieutenant, it doesn't make dying seem so bad. Are you religious?"

"We all are, Captain. We are so close to joining our forefathers I can almost hear them talking."

Thomas smiled and said, "I see your point. This has been a good day, I shall remember it.

Thomas mused, *"I have changed much since coming to war. I used to be tender with people and think of their feelings. Here I am mutilating and killing, and I'm good at it. I wonder what mother or Dr. Phillips would feel if they could see what I do. I hardly know who I am now. I'm a stranger to myself. Who could ever like a person like me if they knew how many people I had maimed or killed? What will I do if I survive the war? Can I ever be tender again? What will I do? I just want to get away from everyone and never hurt anyone again."*

A messenger came and said, "The colonel wants to see you, Captain."

Thomas reported. The colonel said, "Have a seat." Thomas took a seat and the colonel said, "I have bad news. Just a few minutes ago, I was notified that your father has passed away. The war is at a pause at present as it's winter. Take leave and go tend to your mother."

"Thank you, Colonel, I will do that."

There was a pause in the fighting as Lee needed to re-supply his troops, and there was a change in the command with the Union troops. Winter was upon them, so both armies stood down.

Thomas notified his troop that he would be gone on leave, and that Lieutenant Estep would be in charge. He pulled Howard aside and said, "I have to go home, Lieutenant, my father has died and I must tend to my mother."

He left that day and was able to catch a train to New York. It gave him time to reflect on his past. He had loved his dad, but his father had not spent that much time with him. His world was at the bank and society. He knew his mother would miss him, though. His father had spent time with his mother, and was an excellent husband.

He thought, *"What will mother do? With me gone, she may be very lonely. There is Betty Dowd next door, but Betty is a socialite and spends most of her time away from home. I'll talk it over with mother. She may want to go to England. Her two sisters live there."*

CHAPTER 3

A TRIP HOME

Thomas arrived at Union Station about ten in the morning. After collecting his bag, he saw a barbershop close, so he went there and had a shave and a haircut. He also was able to bathe in a backroom and put on a clean uniform. He then went out looking for a hack. As he was waiting, he saw Miss Stone walking by. He was thrilled and called to her. He said, "Miss Stone, Miss Stone."

She stopped and said, "Do I know you?"

"I'm Thomas Benson, Miss Stone, your prize student."

She looked closely and said, "My, you have grown up, but I can still see the resemblance of my little Thomas."

"Do you have time to visit, I would so like to know what happened to you?"

They went to a bagel shop that was nearby. As they sat,

Thomas said, "I told my mother when you taught me, that I wanted to marry you when I grew up."

"You're about seven years too late, Thomas. I'm married with two children. You should have asked me back then. I might have married you, although you were not much older than fourteen," and they both laughed.

"I see you are in uniform. Are you stationed here?"

"No, Miss Stone, I have been granted leave to come bury my father."

"Oh, I'm so sorry. Is your mother okay?"

"I don't know, I just got off the train when I saw you. I will tell you my heart leaped when I saw you. During the wait before and after battles, I sometimes thought of you. I imaged you were my sweetheart and it sustained me."

"I would have thought you would think of Carol Lombard and her kisses," and they both laughed.

"No, Carol was too much for me to handle. I remember how she made the whole class laugh countless times. It was she who got me to kiss her, when you caught us. And she, of course, thought up the drama we performed. Had I married Carol she would have dominated me as she probably now does to her husband."

"Yes, it would be her. She was pretty, though."

"Yes, she was pretty, but you are gorgeous."

"I will have to tell my husband about you.. I'll tell him he must be on his toes, as I now have a suitor. He loves stuff like that, and will enjoy our story. By the way, my name is Stoddard now, Mrs. Michael Stoddard. We live up town. I must be going, I'm meeting my mother."

"They said their goodbyes, and she hugged him and kissed

his cheek, then was gone. Thomas watched her until she was out of site. As Thomas traveled in the hack, he thought, *"I'll have to tell mother that Miss Stone looks just like she always did."*

His mother fell into his arms and cried so hard she shook. She said, "I couldn't have stood it without you, Thomas."

She stood back and looked at him. She said, "I hardly recognized you, son. You have changed so much. Has the war been hard on you?"

"It has, Mother. I have changed and not for the better. I have become hard and bitter. It is hard to explain. I'm a cavalry officer now, and must lead men to their death. I hate it, but that's my job. I try to be the best officer I can. This war has burned my insides out, so much I fear, I will never be what I was again."

"Let's bury your father, then put the sadness behind us, and enjoy each other again. You were not just my son, but the best friend I ever had."

"I feel the same, Mother. However, you gave me some bad advise."

Her brow wrinkled and she said, "How did I do that?"

"You remember Miss Stone?" She nodded, "I ran into her just as I got off the train today. She looks the same as she did when she taught me. I told her that I had told you I wanted to marry her. She laughed and said, 'You're too, late, I've been married seven years and have two children.' Bad advise, mother, those could be my two children."

Matti laughed and said, "It's so good having you with me again."

The funeral went well, Dowd cried so hard that Thomas went over and put his arms around him. Dowd embraced him and cried just the harder. Thomas knew they were close, but didn't realize they were that close.

Many shed tears. Dowd had closed the bank, and all the staff was there with many of them crying. Thomas thought, *"Now that's a heritage. Not many would cry over me if they knew what a killer I've become."*

When they were home, Thomas asked his mother what she planned to do. She said, "Stay here and wait for you."

"I hate to be so negative mother, but we must face reality. There is little chance I will survive the war. I have been very lucky thus far, but I can't see surviving it. It's easier if you count yourself dead. You can do your job much better, because the fear is gone. There's no use fearing what is inevitable. It's hard to listen to this, I know, Mother, but it's true. Plan your life without me, as I can assure you, I won't last another three months."

Matti began to cry and Thomas held her. He said, "Look at the positive side, Mother. God was so generous to let us be together so long. We will have eternity to together in heaven with dad." Her tears subsided, but she clutched him more tightly.

Even though snow was on the ground, they ran together the next day, and it was fun. They had four more days of fun then he left. She did not go to the station with him, as he asked her not to. He said, "It will be easier to part at the house."

CHAPTER 4

RETURN TO THE WAR

On his trip back he thought of Miss Stone and what a joy it would have been to be her husband. When he arrived he reported to the colonel.

The colonel said, "Thomas you arrived just in time. We're moving out of Pittsburg tomorrow. We're heading for Maryland again. Lee is gathering most of his troops and the Union wants to meet him there. We may end the war there, one way of the other. Sometimes I don't care which way, but never repeat that."

Several times he tended men's wounds with great skill. His superiors noticed his talent and asked how he learned to tend wounds.

He replied, I went through medical school before I was taken by the army."

His superiors talked it over about sending him to a medical unit, but Colonel Lewis said, "He's too valuable to us. He leads like a banshee. He's worth five men, and just think, we have a doctor with us at all times."

The others smiled and another colonel said, "Caleb's right. We need him more than they do."

Preparation was now being made for a battle near a small town called Gettysburg. Five roads met at that location, making it strategic to both sides. All the men knew this would be the greatest battle of the war.

As they were preparing for battle, Thomas was sent a message to report to general headquarters.

When he arrived three generals were seated. One said, "We are promoting you to Major, Captain Benson. We want you to take a battalion of men to Vicksburg, Mississippi. We are sending others, but you will be the first. General Grant has requested a division, and we will answer that request, but not all at once. You will be the first to leave with your battalion. Good luck."

Thomas was relieved to know he would not be in the battle of Gettysburg. Over seventy thousand troops were assembled to meet Lee's army.

As they left, Lieutenant Estep said, "That order probably saved our lives."

They traveled by train. They were often stopped as the rails had been removed by rebel forces. It took nearly three weeks. It was the fifth of July when they arrived. The battle for Vicksburg was over. General Pemberton, the commander of the rebel forces, had surrendered the day before they arrived. There were still hundreds of bodies to be buried. As it was warm, the bodies were swollen and the smell from them was atrocious. Thomas had his company commanders organize burial parties. It took three days to bury them.

Thomas reported to General Grant. General Grant said, "You were too late to help us, but I see you took the initiative in burying the dead. I received a letter from your commanding officer saying he was sending me his best officer. That's quite an honor Major Benson."

Three weeks later, Thomas was given orders to take his battalion by ship, back to New York. From there he was to travel south and rejoin his army. The trip was long and the food not so good. It took awhile to organize their march south. Thomas had just time to visit his mother. She was glad to see him. Thomas noticed she was much thinner and he asked her about it.

She said, "I'm under the care of Dr. Bernstein. He said I needed to eat more meat. I guess I have been remiss in eating meat, as I did that to aide the war effort. Don't worry about me."

Thomas left the next day with his troops. He met his division that was assigned to chase the rebels who were in full retreat. There were several engagements. They were ordered to press the enemy at a high cost of men's lives.

At a staff meeting, Thomas asked about that. He was told that the order came from Lincoln, himself. As he could see that the war was almost over, he protected his men the best he could. His commander no longer thought of him as the ferocious man he had been, and subjugated him to a rear mop up force. That was fine with Thomas. He surely would never make the military a career.

Lee surrendered. Thomas was called into headquarters and asked if he wanted to stay in the military. He said, "I would like to be discharged as quickly as is convenient, Sir."

Two days later he was a freeman. As he was now near Richmond, he took a ship back to New York. He was so tired of war, that he just wanted to go someplace away from everyone, and live in solitude.

When he arrived in New York, he decided to have a shave and a haircut before he greeted his mother. He then went to the house. Upon seeing him, one of the long time servants burst into tears and ran to him and hugged him. She had never hugged him before.

She said, "Oh, Mr. Benson. You're too late. Your mother died last week. You must ask Doctor Bernstein for the details.

Thomas was stunned. He decided to bathe and change before he went to see Dr. Bernstein. When he was at the hospital he wanted to look his best. He entered Dr. Bernstein's office and he rose. He just went into Thomas' arms and sobbed. Thomas was dry eyed. He was now too disciplined to show emotion.

He said, "What happened, Doctor?"

She had cancer, Thomas. She had always been so healthy that I thought it was because of her eating habits, that she lost so much weight. There was nothing any of us could do. I'm so sorry."

Thomas had nothing to say, but thanked him for tending his mother. He then turned and went back to his house. He knew there were many things he had to accomplish before he could leave. Lately, he had been thinking of running a few head of cattle in a western state. This would take him away from everyone. He knew nothing about ranching, but thought, *"I can learn. There must be books on the subject."*

He went to the bank and met with Barney Dowd. Barney was emotional as always, but could see Thomas steeled himself, so he went right to the business.

Dowd said, "After your mother's death I went to work on your legacy. I have everything laid out for you. Even I was surprised by your father's wealth. You are a rich man, Thomas. Would you consider going into the banking business?"

"Thank you, Mr. Dowd, but I am going out west. Mostly to be alone. I am so sick of war that I don't want to be around people. I want to get me a piece of land and run a few cattle and be alone."

Please assemble all my assets in an account and be the administrator of that.

"Of course. I will consider it an honor. I will need you to give me a power of attorney to accomplish that. Do you have anyplace in mind that you will be going?"

"Not at this time. I will write you. I will need ten thousand in cash before I leave. Can that be accomplished?"

"Certainly. You can pick it up here tomorrow."

"Good, I will be leaving tomorrow."

As he returned home he thought, *"Dying is as part of life as being born. We all have to do it."* He had been away from his parents so long, it was hard to have emotions, except for his mother.

The next day he returned to the bank and Dowd had his ten-thousand. He thanked him as he was signing papers giving Dowd power of attorney.

Dowd said, "Thomas, I loved your father and mother. If

you ever want to come back, Betty and I will be here for you. Your father made me everything that I am, and I won't forget that. Please write us every three months or so, we will want to know you're safe."

"I'll do that Mr. Dowd. Give my respects to Mrs. Dowd."

He made provisions for transferring money to a another bank where he would be, by using a code word.

He had purchased a map and boarded a train to St. Louis. He was reluctant to talk to anyone, but he decided the only way to learn about the country was to talk to someone from there.

He hadn't brought many clothes as he thought he would wait and see what other men were wearing in the place he landed. He saw a man sitting alone in the diner and asked, "May I join you, Sir?"

"Certainly, young man. I would like your company."

"May I ask where you are from, Sir?"

"I hail from a small village named Ada, Missouri."

"I hate to bother you, but I'm heading out West to start a small cattle ranch. Nothing big, just a few head to sustain me. Is Ada good ranching country?"

The ranching can't be beat, but the war tore up Missouri. Half for the South and half for the North. Brother against brother, families against families. A terrible thing. Were you in the war?"

"Yes."

"Which side?"

"Does it matter, now?"

"No, recon it don't. I like that answer. I wish everyone had your philosophy and would put the war to bed. If you decide to come to Ada, look me up. I'm Cal Seavers. I run a pharmacy there. I didn't catch your name."

"Thomas Benson,"

"I go back East each year to place my orders for the year in person. It gives me a small vacation. I used to take Emily, but the good Lord took her two winters ago. I've never gotten over it. It's a terrible thing."

"I'm sorry Mr. Seavers. I wish I could have known her."

"I'll give you some advice young man. When you see an Emily, do everything you can to marry her. It will turn your life from loneliness to the Garden of Eden."

"I'll take that advice, Mr. Seavers, but few women would have the likes of me. The war burned out my insides, and I don't have much to offer a woman."

"Give her your love, Mr. Benson. Be devoted to her. Love will heal your insides and you'll be a new man."

Mr. Seavers was in another car and Thomas went back to his car. He wanted to find Ada on his map. He found it. It was pretty isolated, so it looked like a place he might like. After all, he already had a friend there.

At the next change of trains, Mr. Seavers and Thomas were sitting close to one another and took their meals together. Cal was loquacious and Thomas only talked when he had to. By the time they crossed the Mississippi they had decided to buy a buggy together and travel to Ada. They would sell it again in Ada.

The trip was easy as the trail was used by a stagecoach. They stayed in the way stations and villages that the stage used. By the time they reached Ada, Thomas knew about everyone in the town of Ada as Cal talked about each one.

Cal had told him about a rancher named Bob Braxton. He owned the biggest ranch near Ada. He was also the major stock holder of the bank and had loaned money from his own account, to several of the merchants to help them get started. He didn't hold a public office, but did control them to a certain extent. Cal hadn't said anything against Braxton, but it was his tone, like he didn't approve of one man having so much influence in Ada.

When they reached Ada, Thomas said, "I will need a buggy here. I would like to buy your half of the buggy and horse," As Seavers lived in town and close to his store, he was more than willing to sell.

Thomas said his goodbyes and went to the only hotel in town. It was austere, but clean. It had a bed, table, bureau and a closet for his clothes. It also had a water closet down the hall with a commode and bathtub.

After getting his things organized, he decided to buy some clothes. He had noticed that most of the men wore levis and western shirts. They all wore cowboy hats.

He went to a general store, and was waited on by a nice looking young lady, who gave him a gorgeous smile. Thomas told her he needed some western clothes like all the men wore around Ada.

She smiled and said, "Are you from back East?"

"Yes. I want to fit in and not be noticed. Will you help me?"

"I won't mention you're from back East, and I'll do the best I can to outfit you, so you'll fit in around here. What do you do, Mr......"

"Benson, Thomas Benson. I'm hoping to buy some land and start a small ranch. Just a few head, nothing big."

"If you stay small enough, I don't think Mr. Braxton will bother you."

Thomas put on an innocent look and said, "Who's Mr. Braxton?"

"He owns the biggest cattle ranch around here and most of the town. You'll know about him soon enough."

"You don't sound like you like him."

"I don't want to leave that impression, Mr. Benson. He's nice enough to me, he just likes to throw his weight around and that galls a lot of people."

"Well, I'll stay out of his way. Is there a land company here in Ada?"

"Yes there is. Herb Anderson owns that. He's located down the street on the left hand side, but you'll have to across the street. He'll treat you right. Tell him that his favorite niece, Lesley, sent you. He's my father's brother."

"I'll tell him Miss Anderson, good day."

As he left Lesley looked out the window until he went into her uncles place. She thought, *"If he would take some of that fur off his face, I bet he'd be downright handsome. I wonder how old he is. He must be less than thirty. He's old enough to settle down. A cattle ranch, sounds like my type of man."*

Lesley's father came up behind her and said, "He's a fine looking man, Lesley. You had better get him before someone else fetches him."

"Oh, daddy, why do you think he would be interested in me?"

"Because you're the sweetest and best looking woman in this town. At least he's better that than Junior Braxton. He's so full of himself that he may burst any day now."

"Well, Junior is the only boy who ever asked me out."

"That's only because he intimidates anyone who goes near you."

"You don't know that."

"Yes I do. Orville Stokes told me."

"Do you believe everything Orville Stokes tells you?"

"Most, I've never known him to lie."

"Well, Mr. Benson may not give me the time of day."

"He will if you'll show an interest."

"Now how would I do that."

"I'll invite him to church. Junior has never set foot in church since his mother had him christened."

"Do that daddy, I like his looks."

CHAPTER 5

ADA

At the land office, Thomas introduced himself. He said, "A nice looking lady told me you were her favorite uncle and would help me."

"My, you are talking about the sweetest girl in the state of Missouri. How may I help you?"

"I want to buy a small spread. Just big enough to run about fifty head of cattle. It must have year-round water and good grass, and I hope it has a house on it."

"I just happened to know a place like that. Jim Rush told me he's selling. He don't want Braxton to have it, so keep that under your hat."

"What does Braxton have to do with it?"

"You're new around here. Braxton owns everything around here or thinks he does. He told Rush that he would like to buy him out. He offered Jim a lowball price. Jim said, he would think about it. Rush is a smart man and knows Braxton. He wants to get out of Ada before anything happens.

"I thought I had better tell you the jest of it, before you put down your money. Do you still want to look at it?"

"Looking at it can't hurt. How far is it?"

"Less than two miles out of town. It's between Braxton's place and town. However, there are steep hills around the place, so Braxton has to ride around it to town. If it's inaccessible to his ranch, why would Braxton wanted it?"

"Maybe for Junior, if Junior ever marries."

The Rush's place was nice. It was approximately six hundred acres surrounded by steep hills except for the river. The river ran through a cut with steep banks. On the place between the ranch and town were small farms. They were fenced and had a road that ran from the Rush ranch to town.

They rode around the place in Anderson's buggy. Thomas said, "There's no need for fences, as natural barriers are on two sides, the river on another and the farmer have fenced off the land in front."

They drove up to the Rush place and Jim came out when he heard them driving up. He said, "Get down and I'll serve you some coffee."

"I've got a potential buyer, Jim."

"Did you tell him about Braxton?"

"I did, Jim."

"I wouldn't sell, unless he knows the straight of it."

They were drinking their coffee and Thomas said, "How much do you want for it, Mr. Rush?"

"Well, I paid two thousand for it. It had this house and the

31

barn. I put in a thousand dollars having a well dug including the windmill, tank and piping. There is about a thousand-feet of fencing to make pastures. I also cleared the land for hay and corn for winter feed. I figure about five-hundred in labor. With the repairs and all, I figure I have about four-thousand in the place. I sell it to you for that. What do you say."

"I think the place is worth ten-thousand, but subtracting Braxton's threat at about six-thousand, I figure four-thousand is a good price." and they all laughed.

"Young fellow, please sleep on it a night. Braxton is a hard man. You could lose your life if he wants this property bad enough."

"I think you're about the best man I ever met, Mr. Rush. How much did Braxton offer you?"

"Two thousand. He knows it's worth much more. I figure he thought he could intimidate me. I think life is too precious to take a chance. If you want to chance it, that's your business."

"If he looks like he might do something rash, I'll sellout at two-thousand dollars. Do you have some livestock you would like to sell?"

"No, everything that's on this property is yours. Joann and I can live quite comfortably the rest of our lives on the four thousand plus my savings. She's always wanted to go back to Liberty where she grew up. She still has some kin there, so that's where we'll be. If you have trouble, please notify me. I still have some friends around here who may help you."

"I thank you for that. Let's close the deal tomorrow. I'll have your money then, but you take all the time you want moving. I'm single and can make out."

Jim looked at Herb and said, "The Lord is so good to me.

At times I nearly cry in gratitude. Joann is in town now. You know, we put this in the hands of the Lord. He blessed us with you, Mr. Benson. We will both pray for you everyday."

They closed the deal the next day. Thomas had the cash. He had brought the ten-thousand dollars in cash with him.

Herb Anderson said, "I'll have it recorded today. You can pick up your copy of the deed tomorrow."

"Thanks, Mr. Anderson."

As Thomas was crossing the street, not fifty feet from him, a man was whipping a Negro with his belt. The Negro was on the ground with his arms over his face to deflect the blows. When the man tired, he kicked the Negro and said, "The next time you don't get off the boardwalk when I'm walking on it, I'll kill you."

With that, the man turned and went into a saloon. Thomas went to the Negro and helped him up. The Negro said, "Please don't help me, Mr. Junior may kill you."

Thomas helped him up anyway and said, "Where do you live?"

"I used to be owned by Mr. Braxton, but he kicked me off his ranch yesterday, whens I asks him for wages. I've been looking for work."

"Well, you just found work at my ranch. I bought the Rush place today. I'll pay you thirty a month and found."

"That's way too much. If Mr. junior finds out, he'll want to whips me, again."

"He won't find out. Just you and I will know. Wait for me at the west end of town by that oak tree. I have to buy some things then we'll ride out in my buggy. By the way, what's your name?"

"Ed, Sir. Ed Bowie."

"You don't have to "sir" me Ed. You're a free man. I spent four years of my life setting you and those like you free, and I'm not above putting my life on the line again for you."

"I's truly grateful, but let's talk when you gets me out of town."

An hour later Thomas picked Ed up in his buggy. As they were driving, Thomas asked, "Do you have a family?"

"I did, but Mr. Braxton, he sold my wife and two children to a man from Texas last year."

Thomas was shocked. He said, "But the war was over before they were sold."

"The war don't have no meanin' to Mr. Braxton. He still has three slaves at his house. They do the cooking, cleanin' and one keeps the barn and chickens."

"Well, I'm not here to make trouble. We'll mind our own business and keep out of trouble."

"Yes Sir."

"Stop that "siring" me, Ed. We're equal, now."

Ed put a big smile on his face.

"Ed do you know where in Texas your wife and children are?"

"I heard Mr. Braxton say the man was livin' around Ft. Worth."

When they arrived at the Rush house. Jim came out when he heard the buggy.

Jim said, "You're just in time for supper. Isn't that Ed Bowie with you?"

"Yes. Braxton fired him yesterday, so I hired him. Will he be welcomed at your table?"

"Yes, if you want him."

"I want him. I risked my life for four years to give people like Ed freedom, and I want to see it in action."

"Oh, no, Mr. Rush, I'll eats out back."

"No you won't, Ed. What Mr. Benson says around here, goes. He bought my place and paid cash money for it. If he says you eat with us, you eat with us."

When they were eating, Thomas asked, "Could you and Joann stay on for another month. Ed and I have to go to Ft. Worth to fetch his family."

"I heard about Braxton selling them, but no one could or would do anything about it. To do so, may have meant Braxton killing someone."

"Is you really going to Ft. Worth for my family, Mr. Benson?"

"We are. We're leaving tomorrow if Mr. and Mrs. Rush will mind the ranch while we're gone."

"We'll do that, won't we Joann?"

"For a worthy cause like that, we'll stay for a year, if it takes that."

Ed and Thomas left the next morning.

CHAPTER 6

FT. WORTH

Rush outfitted them well. They took the buggy and were off.
The trip went well. They followed a stage route to Springfield.
They didn't eat in cafés as they knew the South still had much
bigotry, and they didn't want to cause any trouble.

Out of Springfield, they traveled to Joplin. They stopped
there to get provisions. They were in a general store when
a man said, Major Benson! as I live and breath! Do you
remember me? I'm Howard Estep?"

Thomas said, "I do, Lieutenant Estep. You were by my side
through much of the war. You were an inspiration to us all.
I'm glad we made it through the war. This is my good friend,
Ed Bowie. Ed is helping me build a ranch near Ada, Missouri.
We're riding to Ft. Worth to fetch his family."

Estep put out his hand to Ed. Ed said, "I don'ts feels right shakin' your hand Mr. Estep. But I's thankful to you for setting me free."

"You're who I was fighting for, Ed. Shake my hand and make me proud."

A man behind them said, "You shake that nigger's hand, and I'll put a hole in you."

Estep turned and said, "Make your play, but I warn you, you'll be dead if you do." The man noticed Estep's tied down gun and the gun stance he was in. Estep was staring the man in the face with a frozen look on his face.

The man said, "Another time, maybe."

"No! The time is now! You either apologize or I'll kill you where you stand. I'll even give you the words. Say, 'I'm sorry Mr. Bowie, I misspoke.'"

Thinking that Estep's name was Bowie he said, "I'm sorry Mr. Bowie, I misspoke."

"Say you except his apology, Mr. Bowie."

The man was shocked that the Negro was Mr. Bowie."

"Ed said, "I accepts," and the man whirled around and left."

Thomas said, "This may not be over, if he has some friends. Let's get out of here."

They were out of town ten minutes later. Thomas said, "let's ride all night, I don't want any trouble."

"Okay," Estep said, "My horse is fresh."

They rode all that night and most of the next day. They tied up early as all were worn out. They just ate jerky and went to bed. The sun woke them, and they were off.

As they rode Thomas asked Estep where he was headed. He said, "No where I guess."

"Why don't you come live with Ed and me. I bought a small ranch near Ada, Missouri. I plan on running some cattle. I can pay you thirty a month and found."

"That's beats roaming the countryside. I had nothing left in Illinois, so I just started drifting. You can't believe how I felt when I saw you. You were a sight for sore eyes. I can still see you after that battle in Maryland with blood dripping from your sword and smoke all over the place.

"Sergeant Rimes said, 'Just look at him. I wish every soldier who wears blue could see what an American hero looks like.' Every soldier in our outfit thought you were the epitome of a brave soldier."

They stayed in Tulsa in an abandoned house, as they knew no hotel would take Ed. They rested a full day, then left for Ft. Worth. Thomas watched Ed and he could tell he was nervous.

They reached Ft. Worth and camped a little way out of town. Thomas asked, "What's your wife's name, Ed?"

Ed smiled and said, "Skillet."

This brought smiles to both Howard's and Thomas' faces. Thomas said, "You're not putting me on are you, Ed?"

"No sir. Her daddy named her that."

What are your children's name?"

"Hanna and Emma."

"You stay here. I'll poke around some, and try to learn where they're at."

Thomas went to the stockyards and inquired. The name was so unusual he thought someone would remember. An old timer smiled and said, "Yes, I heard the name. The Hawkins outfit has her. They have a place south of town about three miles.

Thomas thanked the man and returned to where Howard and Ed were. They packed up and were on the road just a half hour later. They met a man coming from a ranch house in a buggy. Thomas asked, "Is that the Hawkins' place, Sir?"

"Yes, I just left from there."

"Do they have a colored woman?"

The man smiled and said, "You mean, Skillet. Yes, they do."

"Thank you," and the man drove away.

Thomas said, "This may be a sticky situation, so let me ride in and see what I can do."

Both men nodded and Thomas took the buggy and rode in. When he came to the house a man came out and said, "Are you here on business?"

"Yes I am. I'm looking to buy a black woman and I hear you have one."

"That depends on the price."

"What do you want for her?"

"She would normally bring fifteen-hundred dollars, but since the war, the price went down quite a bit. I'll take five-hundred."

"Does she have any children?"

"She had two, but one was bit by a copperhead and died. The other is about breeding age, so I'll want seven-hundred for her."

"If they are in good shape, you have a deal."

The man turned around and shouted, "Dorothy, bring Skillet and Hanna out here. I just sold them."

A voice came back saying, "Damn it Harold, I need those niggers."

Harold went over and in hushed tones said, "I got word that a troop of blue bellies are browsing the area. They may find them, and take them for nothing. Don't worry, I'll find some more."

In just a few minutes Skillet and Hanna appeared with a cloth tied around their belongings. They had pitifully little. Thomas told them to get in, and they rode on the backseat. Neither said a word.

As they were driving Thomas said, "You'll be living in Missouri, Skillet. You're going to love it, because you'll be free."

"I'll never be free until I gets my husband back."

About that time, they drew up to the camp. Skillet saw Ed and he saw her. They ran to each other and embraced. It was such a poignant sight that both Thomas and Howard turned their heads to avoid anyone seeing their tears.

Hanna was right behind her mother and they all three were crying and hugging.

Skillet composed herself and said, "Dat man bought us for twelve-hunnerd dollars, then told us we's free. Is he an angel from heaven?"

Howard said, "Yes, he is. I saw this man risk his life countless times for just you, Skillet. I did the same. Seeing your reunion with Ed was worth it all."

Skillet came to Thomas and knelt before him and kissed his hand. Thomas pulled her up and said, "Don't ever bow again to anyone, but Jesus. You're a free woman, as free as the queen of England. Let's go home now."

They avoided Joplin on their way home. It took ten days. When they arrived, Jim Rush had a large smile on his face. He said, "We will have a feast tonight, and celebrate your family, Ed."

Ed took Skillet aside and said, "They'll make us eat with them at the table, Skillet. Just acts like it's natural. Hanna, just look at Mrs. Rush and do whats she dos. You'll be alright."

"I don't knows if I can do it, Papa. I'm so scared my hands are shakin'."

When they were all at the table, Jim said, "I know this is strange for you and Hanna, Mrs. Bowie, but this is how Jesus intended us to be, free and equal. It will take you some time, but you'll get use to it.

"Mrs. Rush and I will be leaving tomorrow and you will be the lady of the house then. You will take your place in this house and live as the white folk do. Mr. Benson said this is your home.

"Ed, will you return thanks."

All bowed their heads and Ed said, "Lord, I is so full of your spirit, I cans hardly talks. Skillet, Hanna and me thanks you for sending your angle, Mr. Benson, to fetch us. He and Mr. Howard puts their lives on the line for usens the entire war. We thanks you for keeping them safe. Bless Mrs. Rush for fixin' this feast. I say the words in the name of your precious son, Jesus. Amen."

The next day Thomas said, "Ed and you will have the back bedroom and Hanna the loft. Me and Howard will occupy the front bedroom. If people come over just act like you are hired help. There are still people who haven't adjusted to the Negroes being free. It will take some time. However,

I can see the time when that will happen. We just have to be patient.

"I'm going to town today and buy some clothes for you. I want you to look good.

Thomas and Howard drove off. When they arrived in town, Howard went to the saloon, while Thomas went to the general store.

Lesley had a large smile on her face when he arrived. She said, "I thought you had pulled stakes on us, until my uncle said you were now the owner of the Rush Ranch.

I guess it's the Benson ranch now. I'm glad you're back. What can I do for you?'

"I brought back some help for the ranch. I found Ed Bowie's wife and daughter and I want to buy clothes for them."

Lesley was shocked and said, "Don't let Braxton know they're working for you. He may take offence."

"Well, he'll know sooner or later. I don't plan on hiding them. Let's see to those clothes."

I know about the size of Skillet, but how big is Hanna, now?"

"She's about the size of her mother. I want good clothes. Not fancy, but good sturdy clothes. I want good shoes and bonnets so they can attend church on Sunday. They'll have to have a good dress for that."

"Mr. Benson you have a heart of gold. Some woman will be lucky to have you."

"Does that include you, Miss Anderson?"

Lesley turned bright red and barely said, "I guess."

"Then I'll call on you Sunday afternoon and take you for a buggy ride. That is, if your father approves."

A voice from the back said, "I approve. I wondered when you would get around to calling on the best looking girl in Missouri who has a heart of gold."

"I'm slow, Mr. Anderson. Your daughter has a project on her hands. I've never been out with a woman. I was in medical school, then the war. I'm twenty-six years old and have never been kissed by anyone but my mother and aunt. I just never had the opportunity, but I see God lead me to Ada, Missouri to make this precious find."

"An unused man, Lesley. That's as rare as my Lesley. You're in good hands with Lesley, you can trust her."

Down at the saloon, Howard was having a drink and was at the end of the bar alone. About that time, Junior came in with three of his crew. He said to the barkeep, "I hear that a stranger bought out Jim Rush."

"I'll have to taunt him into a gunfight. Dad wanted that place for Lesley and me. I'd like to beat dad to the punch and get it myself. I'm the fastest gun in Missouri." With that, he pulled his gun and shot at a picture. Howard saw he was mildly fast, but noticed several things about how he wore is gun and how he eared back the hammer. He knew he could beat him easily, but could Thomas?

He remembered Thomas' quick hands and how he knew no fear. He smiled to himself and thought, *"In three days time, I can have Thomas much faster than that half pint, who thinks he's so tough."*

He finished his drink and walked down to the general store. They put the things Thomas had bought in the back, and went back to the ranch.

Skillet and Hanna were overwhelmed with the clothes.

They both cried, but Thomas said, "You'll earn those clothes, so don't be thanking me." Ed just shook his head and thought, *"Are we in heaven?"*

They were working the next day as the corn needed hoeing. Howard and Thomas took a break and Howard told him about what Junior said in the saloon.

Howard said, "Let me work with you a few days. I can bring you up to snuff. I don't want my food supply to get himself killed off."

Thomas laughed and said, "I've never worn a sidearm except in the war. I always had my pistol out when we were fighting, so I have some to learn."

Howard went to town and bought the hand gun he wanted Thomas to use. He knew guns well, and a colt 38 was the best gun for a fast draw. It had a shorter barrel, and was accurate up to two hundred feet. Larger guns, as the colt 44, had a longer barrel, and had a longer range. However, at a hundred yards everyone used a rifle. There were very few people in the world who could use a rifle as well as Thomas. He could lever shots faster that your eyes could see. He was also deadly accurate.

Howard also bought ten boxes of shells. Lesley said, "I haven't seen you around here. Are you with the Braxton Ranch?"

"No, I'm working for a stranger. I may buy some land around here. It looks like good ranching country."

"Before you do, I would advise you talk to the land agent. He may give you a new prospective."

"I see you aren't sporting a wedding band, are you single?"

"Yes, but I have a boy friend. Actually, two. But one I like and one I don't care for that much."

"Are you spurning me at first sight?"

"No, but I just want you to know how I stand. I hate women who dangle men for their own pleasure."

Howard said, "I think I am falling in love."

Lesley laughed and said, "Tell me your name, cowboy, I don't want all my eggs in one basket."

"Dang, you are something. No wonder Thomas told me to go get a drink when he came to buy the girls clothes."

"You know Mr. Benson?"

"I work for him. I fought beside him for two years and he's the best man you'll ever see. During battle, men would follow him into hell if he asked. You'll find out why if you're around him some."

"My. I've never seen anyone who thought that much of another."

"You've never been in battle where bullets were as thick as a swarm of bees coming at you. I wish you could have seen him after a battle in Maryland. We were looking at Major Benson after that terrible battle and Sergeant Rimes said, 'Have you ever seen the picture of the best soldier that ever wore a blue uniform. Just look at him, and you're seeing him now.'

"If you can catch him, lady, you'll catch the best man you'll ever see. Did you know he drove to Texas to get Ed Bowie's wife and daughter back? He didn't try to bargain with the man, he paid twelve hundred dollars for them."

"Don't you think you're ruining your chances with me?"

"The only way I would have you, Miss Anderson, is if Thomas Benson didn't want you."

"I'm sold. What's your name?"

"I'm Howard Estep formerly Lieutenant Estep of the fourth cavalry." and he clicked his heels.

"Why all the ammunition, Mr. Estep?"

"I just don't like to be running back and forth to town."

"Then I won't be seeing you for about two years."

"No, after seeing you, I'll be back quite often. If you can catch Thomas, I'll get to see you everyday."

The next day Thomas strapped on the gun and scabbard. He was a natural. His hands were so quick, and his aim so straight, that Howard knew he could beat nearly anyone living. However, they practiced everyday.

They were standing side by side, Howard said, "When my hand moves, draw and hit that tree there. It was a four inch sapling. Howard's hand moved and Thomas had fired and hit the tree before Howard's gun was level.

Howard shook his head and said, "You're ready for anyone who goes up against you. Remember look at their eyes. The eyes give away the draw. They will squint."

"Have you killed a man before in a gunfight?"

"Howard said, "I hate to admit it, but I have. I was forced into one in Springfield, Illinois. I now wish I had eaten crow, and told him I was a coward. But, pride got the best of me. I swore that would be the last time I drew on a man. But as fate would have it, not a week later, two men rode up to where I was camped, and asked my name. I said it, and they both drew. I killed both out of reflex. Since then, I've wished that I would have let them kill me.

"I wanted to lose myself, then I saw you. It was like the heavenly chorus started singing. I don't feel alone anymore."

"Well, let's hope the killing is over for us, Howard. I feel better now that you are here. I feel better because Ed, Skillet and Hanna are here. We have a family, Howard."

"We surely have, Thomas."

CHAPTER 7

THE FIGHT

Nothing happened for awhile. Thomas saw Lesley fairly often. She made all the moves, as she knew she would have to. She thought, *"I love him dearly."* She smiled to herself and thought, *"I don't know if I love him as much as Howard does, but I love him."*

Junior was seeing a new saloon girl named Sara. She was a looker and Junior liked her a lot. He told his crew to not go near her."

"However, a cowboy, name Buddy Doolin, from miles away, came to the saloon on a night that Junior was out at the ranch. He saw Sara and she liked him. He had manners and treated her right. The next night Sara was dancing with Buddy with her eyes closed and holding him close, when Junior came in. He was outraged.

He knocked Sara to the floor with his fist, then pounced on Buddy. Buddy could fight, and he began beating Junior to an inch of his life. Junior had never had someone oppose him, because they knew his father coddled Junior, and would have anyone's head who hurt him. The rest of his crew just watched, enjoying Junior get his butt kicked badly.

Junior was unconscious and the boys took him back to the ranch. meanwhile, back in town, some of the men enlightened Buddy about Bob Braxton, Junior's father. They told him what Braxton was liable to do to him if he stayed around.

Buddy did the prudent thing and lit out. He left going east, but circled around and went southwest. He decided he had seen enough of Missouri and headed for Texas where his folks lived.

When they took Junior to the house, Bob said, "Who did this to him?"

Lefty said, "A stranger. He was dancing with Sara, that new whore at the saloon, when we came in. Junior went wild. He knocked that whore to the floor and lit into this cowboy like he wanted to kill him. The cowboy was smaller than Junior, but he apparently knew how to fight. He did up Junior like you see him."

"Why didn't you help?"

Rudy said, "It was a fair fight, boss, and Junior started it. We didn't feel it would be fair if we butted in."

"Fair! Fair! This is my boy you're talking about. You're all fired. I'll pay you off now." He went back and got the money, while his two women servants tended to Junior. The three hands were, Lefty, Rudy and Lester.

As they were riding away from the ranch, Lefty said,

I would have paid the money Braxton paid us, to see that cowboy mop up on Junior. I enjoyed every blow."

Rudy said, "I halfway knew we would be fired, but I wouldn't have broke that fight up for ten jobs."

Lester said, "I liked the way he kept hitting Junior in the mouth. He must have broken three or four of his front teeth out. His lips were a bloody mess. I lived with every blow. I bet he broke several of his ribs. I was hoping one would pierce his lung, but as luck would have it, none did."

Bob took Junior to Springfield where they had a dentist. Junior was in terrible pain. Not only was there excruciating pain from the nerves in his teeth, but his ribs hurt nearly as badly.

The dentist was able to dig out the roots of front teeth and then made him false ones.

The doctor wrapped his ribs, but they still hurt with every breath he took.

They stayed in Springfield for three weeks. Junior ate a lot of soup, as it took him awhile to get used to the false teeth.

It was a week before Bob asked, "What happened Junior?"

I came into the saloon, and some cowboy was dancing with my girl. She was draped around him like she was in love. I don't know what came over me, but I lit into that cowboy. I wanted to kill him with my bare hands. He was a little feller, but he knew how to fight. It didn't take me but a second to know I was in big trouble. I guess he wopped me pretty good."

"Why didn't the boys help you, Junior?"

"I guess they saw it as a fair fight. I hated to get beat so badly in front of them. I'll make it up to them, when we get home."

"You can't do that, Junior. I fired them, and told them I would shoot them if I saw them in Ada again."

"They weren't at fault, dad. I wish you hadn't have done that. They were my only friends. The other hands stay away from me. Now what I am I going to do? By the way, I like that saloon girl a lot. I told her once I would marry her, but she just laughed. I meant it though. I really like her."

"She's a whore, Junior. You can't bring a whore out here. What would people say?"

"They wouldn't say anything, because they know I would kill them if they did."

"You like her that much, that you would marry her?"

"Well, maybe not marry, but I would keep her until I grew tired of her."

"Well, keep her in town. I don't want her out at the ranch. I have a reputation to uphold."

"What reputation is that. Ma ran off with that salesman, and never came back. I figured when the salesman got tired of her, she would come home, but she never did."

Bob was thinking about the whore named Sara. He would pay her a visit and give her three hundred dollars to leave, then he'd be rid of her.

When they returned to the ranch, everything went well for awhile. Then Sara left one day. Junior asked about her, but one of the girls said, "She told me she was going to Texas to find that cowboy. He told her where his folks lived."

"If I know Texas folks, she's not in for grand reception," and they all laughed.

"When Junior found out Sara had ran off to Texas to find

that cowboy who had beaten Junior so badly, he asked, "Do you know what town she was headed for?"

None of the girls could remember and told Junior so. However, everyone of them knew the town's name.

As Lesley was going to the post office, Junior spied her. He walked over and said, "I have been remiss not calling on you, Lesley."

Lesley was nice, but ice cold. She said, "Rumor has it that you were in love with a girl over at the saloon."

"Who told you that?"

"I won't tell, because you would cause them trouble. You're wicked, Junior, and I won't see you again."

"You won't will you. Maybe your daddy and uncle may just lose their businesses if you don't."

"Now that really makes me like you, Junior. You threaten everyone who dares to cross you. You'll get your comeuppance when your daddy isn't around to clean up your messes."

With that, Junior slapped her so hard that she went down. Howard was just coming out of the barbershop when he saw Junior slap her down. He yelled at Junior, "If you walk off from that girl, I'll gun you down where you stand."

Junior squinted at him as Howard took a gunfighter's stance."

Junior said, "Do you know who I am?"

"Yes, you're a fellow who's about to meet Jesus. I will advise you to pick up that woman gently and apologize to her."

Junior had never seen this guy before, but knew that the man was speaking the truth. He wheeled around and picked Lesley up and said, "I apologize, Miss Anderson, but this isn't over."

"Then fill your hand, big mouth."

Junior wheeled around and went to his horse, then rode off toward his ranch.

Everyone had heard all the conversation as their voices were loud.

Junior reached the house and said, "I talked to Lesley Anderson today."

His father smiled and said, "That's who I wanted you to marry, Junior."

"She insulted you and me. I put her in her place though. Do the Anderson brothers owe anything to your bank, Dad?"

"No, they paid off their loan last year, why."

"I was hoping we could foreclose on them and take their businesses."

"You are upset. What did Lesley say to you?"

"She said she heard rumors of me going with a saloon girl and that she would never see me again. I would like to get that little bitch up here and let all our hands have her."

"She's just one girl, Junior. There are plenty of girls in Missouri. Why don't you go over to Springfield and kick up your heels and forget Lesley Anderson."

"It wasn't just Lesley. There was a cowboy there with a tied down gun. He told me that if I didn't pick up Lesley and apologize he would gun me down. I could tell he was a gunfighter, so I went over and picked Lesley up, apologized and then rode off."

"Why was she on the ground?"

"Because I slapped her down when she told me she would never have anything to do with me, again."

Bob began to realize what Junior had become. He thought,

"I'm to blame for Junior, it's all my fault. I spoiled him, and now it's too late to change him. Someday he will go too far, and some cowboy will gun him down. I know it's coming."

Junior wanted to hurt someone. He decided to burn down the general store. Then Lesley would be out on the street with no place to go."

He waited until midnight, then went to the barn and got five gallons of kerosene. He saddled his horse in silence, and led him out the front gate before he got in the saddle. He rode into town, and left his horse at the outskirts. He carried the kerosene to Anderson's general store and poured it all around the store, and especially on the board walk and front door. He then lit it and carried the five gallon bucket to where his horse was tied. There he threw the can into a washed out place. He stayed until the flames were leaping up to the roof and rode off. He was hoping Lesley and her father would burn up with the store.

Lesley was awakened by the roar of the fire. She looked up and the whole room was aflame. She instinctively ran for her window, as the front of the store was engulfed in flames. The only thing that saved her was she liked fresh air at night, and had left the window ajar. She raised the window and climbed out just as the roof fell in behind her. Her nightshirt was afire, but she quickly extinguished it.

She then thought of her father who was in the back bedroom. She knew he was gone, because the roof had caved in on all the store. She just stood there in her nightshirt and was in total shock. The whole building was engulfed, and the walls were now folding in on the building.

Several people had arrived. Lesley explained how she

barely had escaped the flames. They could see her nightshirt was singed where she had beat out the fire.

Her uncle was now beside her, and she fell into his arms and cried. He took her to his house and made some coffee. He said, "There's nothing we can do. You can live with me and help me with my business. I'm sure a pretty face like yours will help the business."

Lesley was sipping her coffee and said, "This was Junior's doings."

"Yes, I believe it was, but there's no way of proving it. However, everyone saw him slap you down, and that stranger make him eat crow. Did you know that stranger?"

"His name is Howard Estep and he's Thomas' best friend. He works for Thomas and is devoted to him. They served in the war together.

"He was in the store when I met him. I wish you could have heard him describe Thomas after a battle in Maryland. The look in his eye was like that of a disciple looking at Christ. He's completely devoted to Thomas. Thomas led him and his company in several battles. I understood more about Thomas, as Howard described him.

"I think Howard would have killed Junior had not Junior did everything he told him. I think Junior felt that, too. That's why he did everything Howard told him to the letter.

"Junior was humiliated. I think that brought on the hate for me. He had to strike back and he went for the easiest target. He's a coward at heart, but is ruled by his urges. He is a slave to them. His father made him that way by coddling him to the point that he's completely selfish.

"I don't think Howard will tell Thomas about Junior slapping me, because he knows Thomas would kill Junior.

"I need to go out and tell Thomas about the store before someone else does. He will just know Junior did it. I know Bob Braxton. He will do anything to protect Junior.

"When Bob's wife ran off with that salesman, he turned all his love toward Junior. That was the worst thing he could do for Junior. I think he can see what he's done now, but it's too late, Junior is ruined. Someone will kill him, soon. I just hope it isn't Thomas for his sake.

"He told me that he's haunted by all the men he killed in the war. He said some of them were only boys, but he had to do it. I think that's why he took Ed Bowie.

"Did you know he went all the way to Texas to find Ed's wife and daughter? I think that was part of the war to him, freeing the slaves. He did that to prove what he fought for. Thomas is deep, Uncle Herb?"

"I know he is. He's quiet, but when he says something, it's worth hearing. I'll take my buggy and drive you out to see Thomas tomorrow morning, Lesley. I'll reinforce what you say. I don't want Thomas to go gunning for Junior, either. I guess Thomas has touched all our lives. I think I love him, too."

"You love him because I love him, Uncle Herb. You're as devoted to me as daddy was. I often thank God for giving me two fathers"

CHAPTER 8

THE FIRE

When they arrived at Thomas' ranch, they were met by Ed and Skillet. They both had smiles on their faces. Ed said, "Please get down. We have coffee for you. Mr. Estep taken Mr. Benson to Springfield to buys some cattle.

"Mr. Estep was insistent that we needs more cattle, and Springfield was where to gets 'em. They taken off early this morning."

Lesley turned to Herb and said "Howard was getting Thomas away from Ada. That trip will take a week. Howard wants to break the news about Junior slapping me while Thomas is miles away. He knows Thomas as well as anyone, and thinks he is protecting him. He won't tell him until he sees Springfield. He thinks he can talk to him and calm him down before they return. You see, Howard loves both of us."

"That was pretty smart. I don't see Thomas as anyone who would have a knee jerk reaction, but if anything could bring that on, Junior slapping you, would bring it."

Lesley said, "Let's have coffee with Ed and Skillet.:

"Oh no, Miss Lesley, we don'ts means we'd sits down and have coffee with you, I'll just fix it for you. I have some sweet things for you, too."

"You're going to have coffee with us, Skillet. We want to talk to you. We have things to discuss."

Ed said, "She means we don'ts feels right about sittin' with you and Mr. Herb."

"You'll just have to get used to it, Ed. We want to visit with you, and like I say, we have some things to tell you."

Reluctantly, Ed and Skillet sat with them at the kitchen table. Lesley told about the fire and losing her father. She said, "I think what brought it on was I told Junior off and he slapped me so hard, I fell to the ground. Howard was coming out of the barbershop just as he hit me. You know Howard. He told Junior if he wanted to live, he would help me up and apologize to me. Junior surely didn't want to do it, but he knew his life was over if he didn't.

"After helping me up and apologizing, he got on his horse and rode to his ranch. Last night I think he took kerosene and put it all around our store and burned it up with daddy in it. I barely got out as the roof caved in. I was singed, but not burned. We could smell kerosene quite strongly this morning, when we surveyed the fire looking for daddy.

"All we found were some of his bones and his skull. The coroner took them and we are having the burial tomorrow.

I hope you will come and bring Hanna. I want you there to represent Howard and Thomas."

"We's be there Miss Lesley. Mr. Benson left the buggy for us."

* * *

When Thomas and Howard were having a beer in Springfield, Howard told Thomas about Junior slapping Lesley."

Thomas said, "That's why we're in Springfield, Howard. You wanted me days away from Ada when you told me. You did right. I would have gunned Junior down that day and a war would be on between Bob Baxter and us.

"You look out for me like an old mother hen."

"Well, it's my turn. You kept me alive during the war and I going to keep you alive after. However, we do need the cows, if we're going to make a living."

"Thomas said, "I never knew the value of friends, until I met you and Ed. During the war, I had no friends nor wanted any. War is a lonely place. It's a place for killing and nothing else. I was dedicated to the war. I understood why were fighting.

"The biggest reason was to preserve the Union and the Constitution. But a more reverent reason, was to give all those colored people freedom. You know, Ed told me he could not only feel freedom, but he could taste and smell it, too. I understood his meaning, but knew I could never smell and taste it like the Negroes. It carved a place in my heart and drove me on to do the best fighting I could.

"Ed is the first Negro I ever knew, but I knew the hearts of those yearning to be free. It's nice to feel I had a part in that. Some men told me they can't live with the faces of those they killed.

"I never saw faces when I fought. I just saw images of the enemy. I had no hate for them, it was like hunting a vicious bear. It was just a job that had to be done. I try not to think of those men. If I did, I don't know if I could live with it. I tried not to keep count of the men I killed, but I did. I killed sixty-seven that I knew of, some that I wounded could have died later. I got superficial wounds, but never was struck a direct blow or had a bullet pierce me. I had some burn me a couple of times.

"I think God kept me alive to mend the wounds of our people."

"Yes, you were quite good at that. You took a bullet out of my shoulder if you remember. I was ready to fight again two weeks later. You have the hands of great surgeon. Why didn't you follow that after the war?"

"I wanted to get away from people. I wanted to be alone and not see anyone. Then I met Ed and later you. You both have made my life whole again."

"When are you going to marry Lesley, Thomas?"

"As soon as we get back. I think her father wanted me to marry Lesley more than Lesley. She told me that once on a buggy ride. I told her I liked him, but was not in love with him. She really laughed. I love to hear her laugh. I try to think of things that are funny to her, just to hear her laugh. I love her deeply. I never had a relationship with a woman before

Lesley. If I had any inkling how wonderful a woman is, I might have been a womanizer."

"No, Thomas, a womanizer just uses women. You love Lesley's soul. I can see it in your eyes when you look at her. I can hear it in your voice, when you talk about her. It brings joy to me to see you and Lesley love one another."

"You're a deep fellow, Howard. I value our friendship a little deeper, now. God again has touched me, bringing me such a good friend.

* * *

Junior had risen early. He didn't want anyone to know he burned down Anderson's store. He was out in the barn doing some chores when the foreman of the crew, named Rowdy James, came in. He was surprised to see Junior working.

Rowdy said, "My, you're up early, Junior."

"Yeah, I went to bed early and woke up early, and have a lot of energy today."

After meeting Rowdy, he felt he had established himself with the crew, and went to the house. He was having breakfast when his father came in.

He said, "You're up early, Junior."

"Yeah, I went to bed early and woke up early. I went out to the barn first to gather some eggs. I really feel good today. Maybe I'll make a habit of going to bed early."

"Are you going to town today?"

"No, I think I'll work with the crew. I haven't done that in awhile and maybe I should. After all, you won't be here forever. I need to get a good work habit."

Bob thought, *"If he worked an hour a day it would be a good work habit. I think I'll follow him around and see what he's up to. I don't quite trust him. He must have a reason for his this."*

Junior left, and Bob finished his breakfast, then walked out onto the front porch. He had just sat down when he saw a delivery wagon coming. The wagon pulled up and the man making the delivery was bringing the boxes to the house. He greeted Bob and then said, "Anderson's store burned down last night. The girl got out, but old man Anderson was caught in the fire. A terrible thing. He was really liked."

"How did the fire start, Homer?"

"There was a strong smell of kerosene. Folks think someone set the fire. It burned so quickly, it seems likely someone poured kerosene all around the house, then lit it."

Bob was stunned. He threw the rest of his coffee off the porch and headed for the barn. He saw that one of the five gallon cans used to transport kerosene to the house was missing. He saddled his horse, and left for town. He always took men with him, but this time he wanted to be alone.

He traveled slowly looking for the kerosene can. He went off the trail several time to look in gullies. He was at the edge of town and went over to a ditch and there lay the can. He picked it up and turned around heading for the ranch.

When he returned he set the can on the porch. He got himself some coffee and sat on the porch. He knew Junior wouldn't work too long. He was right, before he had finished his coffee, he could see Junior riding toward the house. Some rose bushes hid the kerosene can from where the horse hitch was.

Junior walked up the steps and saw the kerosene can. He looked at his father and said, "Why is that can out here?"

"You know why. You burned down Anderson's store last night. It burned up Anderson, but his daughter survived. They'll be coming for you, Junior. Someone may have seen you."

Before he thought, he said, "No one saw me."

"Then you admit burning the store down?"

"Let me tell you what happened, then you tell me what you would have done. Yesterday I talked to Lesley, and told her I wanted to start seeing her again.

"She said that she had heard about the saloon girl, Sara, and would never see the likes of me again. I lost my temper and slapped her. I guess I slapped her pretty hard and knocked her down. I turned and was going to my horse when this cowboy braced me. I could tell he was a gun hand by the way he wore his gun tied down. He was in a gunfighter's stance.

"He told me if I didn't pick Lesley up and apologize to her, he would kill me where I stood. I knew he would, so I picked her up and apologized. I then rode to the ranch. I looked back, and saw that bitch smiling at me as I rode. I won't take that. I thought about it for hours, and the more I thought, the madder I got. If I couldn't have that bitch, no one would. So I burned her out. I didn't think anyone would be killed. That just happened accidental."

Bob sat there awhile then said, "I ought to hang you myself, but I won't. You're all I have. I wish you could change, but I don't think you will."

"I will, Pop, just give me a chance. You saw this morning how I went to work. I got tired and came home as I missed a night's sleep. If you will get me out of this, you'll see, I'll change. I'll work everyday just like the crew. I'll stay away from town, I promise. Just help me this one time."

"I'll give you that chance Junior, but if you go back to your old habits, I won't stand by you. This is your last chance. Now, take that can back to the barn, then get some rest. I'll expect you up before six tomorrow morning, and I want a full days work out of you everyday."

"You'll never be sorry, Pop. I'll change, you'll see."

Junior left and Bob thought, *"He might just change. Maybe what he did will change him. I just hope it does. I'll ride into town later today and see what I can do. I'll put up the money for a new store. Ada needs that store. That's what I'll do. I'll tell Joe to make it look like he's doing the loaning, but leak the fact that I'm behind it. I'll see that Lesley has the deed at a low mortgage rate. I may become a hero out of this."*

That afternoon he rode to town and talked to his banker, Joe Brooks. He said, "Joe, that was a damn shame about the store. Did they find out what started it?"

"Someone poured kerosene all around the store and set it afire. Everyone thinks Junior did it."

"That's absurd. I was with him until late last night playing a card game. We all went to bed late, but this morning Junior was up early and worked with the crew. Did Anderson have any enemies"

"Not that I know of. He was well liked."

"You don't suppose his daughter was mad at him and set the fire."

"She loved him, Bob. You could see it."

"Well, no one can say that for sure. I think Sheriff Ruffins should question her, and maybe even his brother, Herb."

"What motive would they have. The store is gone, and so is her livelihood. His brother has a thriving business."

"What about that new guy who bought Rush's place. He was sweet on Lesley. Maybe her old man didn't like him and made him mad."

"I understand he went to Springfield to buy some cattle."

"Maybe he did that for an alibi."

"You're grasping at straws, Bob. Are you covering up for Junior. He's the prime suspect."

"I told you he was with me. Are you calling me a liar?"

"Of course not Bob. I'm just telling you the facts. Sheriff Ruffins will want to talk to Junior. Everyone is really upset about this."

"Well, that will resolve itself. Let's think of what we have to do."

"What do you mean?"

"We have to have a general store. We must start rebuilding immediately. Why don't you go talk to Lesley and tell her the bank wants to loan her the money at an extremely low rate, and start rebuilding the store immediately. I'll back the whole project."

"Sounds like a good plan. I'll go see her this evening. I understand she's staying with her uncle."

"Keep my name out of it, for now."

That night Brooks called on Lesley. He explained that Ada had to have a store, and they wanted her to start rebuilding immediately. He would find her a builder and handle things from that end. He wanted her to start an inventory, so that all the merchandise would come the minute the structure was finished.

He said, "You'll need a bigger store, I'd say twice the size as the old one. Ada is growing and the store should grow with it."

"I'll think about it, but right now I would say, no. I will be getting married soon and I can't see how a store would fit into that. I will talk it over with my fiancé. He's solid and may want to take that on."

"We'll that is better than a 'no.' Thanks for your time, goodnight to you both."

CHAPTER 9

RETURN OF A WARRIOR

Thomas and Howard returned with thirty head of heifers and two nice bulls. As they road up, Ed had the gate to the corral open and a big smile on his face. He said, "I's sure glad you's back. I feels naked when you's away. I guess I'll always feel I'm a slave. I likes being owned by you, Mr. Benson."

"You're not owned by anyone and you know it. We're just close friends. I missed you, too, Ed. You, Skillet and Hanna are part of my family, now. I hope we can find a good husband for Hanna, so our family will keep growing. Her children will feel like my grandchildren."

Ed waited until they were in the house having some coffee before he told them about the fire. Both Howard and Thomas had gray faces. Neither said anything.

After awhile, Howard said, 'Junior.' I'm going to kill him."

"Now who's going off halfcocked. Let's see the facts and then make a rational decision before we hang him." That made Howard laugh.

Thomas said, "It's nearly dark now. Let's clean up, eat Skillet's delicious diner, get a good night's rest and go in tomorrow morning."

The next morning they were in town by eight. They went to Herb Anderson's house and they were eating breakfast. Lesley jumped to her feet and was in Thomas' arms immediately. She cried her heart out as Thomas held her.

Herb poured them coffee and Lesley said, "I guess you saw the store and heard about dad."

"Yes, Ed told us."

"Joe Brooks came around the next day and told me that everyone wants me to rebuild. He said he would front the money as Ada has to have a store, and the only person they want running it is me.

"I told them that I would discuss it with my fiancé. No one knew we were engaged, not even you, but we are. I'm going to be your wife. I think the wedding will be next Saturday at the church."

Thomas said, "That sounds like a great idea. I know who will stand up for me, but who will stand up for you."

"I've already thought of that. I want Hanna to be my maid of honor. It will shock most people, but it will give Hanna some standing in the community. If we do the store, I will want her to work there as a clerk."

"I'm shocked, Lesley. I think you made a great decision. Hanna's part of my family and I want everyone to know it."

"Then it's set. I'll start making the plans immediately. I won't tell anyone about Hanna until she walks in with me."

"Another good idea."

"Now about the store?"

"If you want to do it, I'll help you. Howard can run the ranch. He and Ed can handle that. Does that sound alright to you, Howard?"

"Sure, Ed and I can handle that easily."

Lesley had a worried face when she said, "What are you going to do about Junior, Thomas?"

"Nothing right away. I'm going by the sheriff's office and see what he has to say."

"I will be swearing out a warrant for his assault on you, Lesley, with Howard's help."

"We'll then see if the sheriff is in Braxton's pocket."

"Be careful, Thomas, I can't have my fiancé getting into trouble."

Howard and Thomas left and found Ruffins at his office. The sheriff rose and said, "I was going to ride out and see you, Mr. Benson."

"I'm investigating the fire that took Mr. Anderson's life."

"Yes, it was a terrible thing. My fiancé was telling me about it. She said she barely escaped with her life."

With a surprised look on his face Ruffins said "You're engaged to Lesley Anderson?"

"Why so surprised, Sheriff? You know she has good judgment."

"Braxton asked me to look at you as a possible suspect."

"Yes, he would. You and everyone else know that Junior

set that fire. If you don't follow that up, the citizens of Ada will run you out of town."

The sheriff slumped in his chair looking depressed. Thomas said, "We're here to swear out a warrant on Junior Braxton for assault and battery against Lesley Anderson. There are several witness, with Howard Estep, here, being an eye witness."

The sheriff again was shocked. He had heard a little about the confrontation, but passed it off, as no one ever confronted Junior for fear of his father, and his many hired hands.

The sheriff begrudgingly wrote out the arrest warrant, and both Thomas and Howard signed it.

"When will you be serving it, Sheriff?"

"I'll ride out this afternoon. I'll have to have Judge Reynolds sign it. He's probably at the saloon by now."

They rode back to Herb's place to tell them the news.

*   *   *

Bob Braxton had already rode back to his ranch, and was sitting on the porch having his coffee, when he saw the sheriff from afar. He went back in and had his maid to pour another cup of coffee for the sheriff. As the sheriff rode up, and tied his horse he had a grime look on his face.

Bob said, "Did you question that stranger that bought the Rush place, Sheriff?"

"Yes. He's going to marry Lesley next Saturday, so I don't think he had anything to do with it. However, he and a man named, Howard Estep, swore out a warrant on Junior for assault and battery. They have witnesses to the assault. Junior knocked Miss Anderson to the ground with his fist. Judge Reynolds signed it, and there will be a trial. Is Junior around?"

"Hold on there Ruffins. You can't ride out here and arrest my boy. He told me about it. Lesley said some bad things to him, and he just took appropriate action. A man can't have a woman talk like that to a man without getting what she deserves."

"Well, that may be the way you and Junior look at it, but the law says it's assault and battery, and if he is convicted he will spend some time in jail."

"I won't have it. You hold your job because I backed you. If you arrest Junior, I won't back you anymore. Do you hear?"

"I hear, but I have to arrest him whether you back me or not. It's the law."

"Be damned the law. What I say goes. You just ride back to town and tell the judge it was just a misunderstanding. Junior said he helped her back up and apologized. What else is expected of him?"

"I don't know, Bob. Let me take him to town and then Judge Reynolds can let him go tomorrow morning. Don't make this worse than it is. The worse case would be Junior spending one night in jail. That won't hurt him."

"Well, Junior is out working with the crew. He won't be back until sundown. I'll send him into you after he cleans up. Is that good enough?"

"I suppose it will have to be. Make sure he rides in." With that said, the sheriff left.

Junior arrived few minutes later. He had seen the sheriff ride up and hid in the barn until he left.

When Junior walked up Bob said, "What are you doing here?"

"I have a headache and didn't feel well. I saw the sheriff ride up, what did he want?"

He has a warrant for your arrest on assault and battery charges. It's about you knocking Lesley to the ground. It's all legal. You need to clean up and ride in. Judge Reynolds will let you go in the morning."

"I won't do it. I helped her up and apologized, and that's all I'm going to do. If he wants me, he'll have to take me."

"Don't be pig headed about this, Junior. If you don't take care of it now, it could get bigger."

"Give me five-hundred dollars, Pop. I think I will clear out for a year or so, and let this blow over. If they jail me, they may try to pin the burning of the store on me. Not many people like me in Ada, and may enjoy putting a noose around my neck. I need to get out of here."

Bob thought a minute and the more he thought of it, the better it sounded. He could say that Junior had to take care of his teeth in Springfield, as he had a terrible toothache."

Before Junior left Bob said, "Did you know that Benson is marrying Lesley Anderson Saturday?"

"This shocked Junior. He said, "She took that stranger over me? I'm glad I burned her store. I just wish she'd been in it."

Bob then knew he had made a good decision. Junior would never change. He was a vicious, spoiled kid. Yes, he was a kid although twenty-two years old. Life would be better with him gone.

Junior left to pack while Bob went to his safe for the

money. Junior said, "I'd like to take the surrey, as I need to pack most everything I have."

"Okay, it looks like rain and you'll need to put up the cover if it does."

When Junior was in the barn hitching up the surrey, his eyes caught a glimpse of the five gallon kerosene can. He filled it, and put it in the surrey. He took another five gallon can that looked like the first, and put it where the other had stood. He drove off about three that afternoon. He had taken his Winchester and several boxes of shells.

He knew of a camping spot not a mile from the Benson's ranch. He had used it several times when hunting. He thought he would go there and make a camp. Saturday was just two days away. It was Thursday and he would make camp and look around for some deer.

The Benson place was just over a hill that acted as a barrier for Benson's livestock. However, Junior knew a trail over the hill. It was steep, and you had to dismount and pull your horse, but it was doable.

He made camp for the night and slept late the next morning. He walked over the mountain to have a view of the house where Benson lived.

That night he made the preparation's for his work Saturday. He thought, *"They will probably leave the niggers at home. No one would want niggers at a wedding."* He smiled and thought, *"I'll kill all his niggers and then he'll have to do the work. I may have some fun with that Hanna before I kill her."*

At about noon, Saturday, Junior was under a tree on the hill. He saw their buggy leave. He couldn't tell who was there, but he did see the gunfighter, who made him apologize, ride off on his horse following them. A thought then crossed his mind. *"If he waited. Benson an Lesley wouldn't return with them, as they would be going on their honeymoon. He could sneak in and kill the gunfighter then kill Ed and Skillet. He would then have some fun with Hanna before cutting her throat. He would put them all in the house and burn it along with the barn."*

He went down to the house, and it was empty. They had taken the Negros with them. He then hid his kerosene and waited in the barn. They would come to the barn first. That's when he would kill the gunfighter, then the niggers.

About five that afternoon he saw the three Negroes returning, but no sign of the gunfighter. What had happened was, Howard had gone to the saloon to have a few drinks and make a night of it.

When they drove up to the barn, Junior stepped out and said, "I'm not here to hurt anyone, I just came to talk with Benson. Acting innocent he said, "Where is he?"

"He done got married today Mr. Junior. We's all that is here."

"What about that gunslinger?"

"He wents to the saloon to have a few drinks. He probably won't comes home until late."

"Well, I don't want any trouble from you. Tie up your woman and Hanna, and tie them tight. I don't want no one running off."

Ed minded, and tied them up. When they were tied, Junior turned the gun on Ed and shot him. He then turned the gun on Skillet and shot her. He then turned to Hanna and said, "Now, we're going to have a little fun. He raped her, then slit her throat. He pulled them into the house and drenched it with kerosene, then lit it afire.

There was enough kerosene left to burn the barn, so he headed there. He ran the livestock out and set it afire. Back at his camp, he ate, had a smoke, then packed up and left. It was now dusk, but he knew the way and pulled out for Springfield.

Howard had three or four drinks and then left. As he was riding home, he could see the glow of the fire. He ran his horse as fast as it would go. When he arrived, the house and barn were burned to the ground. He saw the kerosene can and knew who had done it. Not seeing the Bowie family, he knew they were dead.

Howard had also scouted the area looking for game, and knew of the trail over the mountain. There was no other way for Junior to go. He pulled his horse over the trail and then mounted and headed for the camp. It was vacant, but showed signs of being used recently. There was only one trail and that led to Springfield. That would be where Junior would be going. He rode on and could see the buggy up ahead.

He knew Junior would have to camp somewhere, so he just stayed behind him about three hundred yards. The moon wasn't so bright, so he stayed just far enough behind to see if he stopped. In another twenty minutes the buggy turned off the trail.

Howard tied his horse by a stream so it could drink, and then went on foot. He watched Junior stop at a place near the same stream. He walked into Juniors camp and said, "Don't try anything, Junior, or I'll shoot you in both knees. I don't want you to die. I'm taking you to your father's house."

This was good news to Junior. He knew his father would protect him rather that help the gunfighter.

Howard said, "Tie your feet together." Junior followed his instructions. Howard then walked over and tied his hands behind his back. He threw him in the buggy and tied his horse behind the surrey.

They left and drove toward the Braxton's ranch. While they were traveling Howard thought of how to handle Braxton's dogs. He stopped when he saw the arch over the gate and dug through Juniors grub box. He found what he was looking for, fresh meat.

He then gagged Junior. He traveled onto the large gate that had a wrought iron arch over it. He opened the gate and two dogs came running. He threw them the meat. They smelled Junior and didn't bark.

Howard then drove the surrey just under the gate. He took his rope and made a hangman's noose. He came around and said, "Junior we're going to a party. It's a hanging party and you're the guest of honor."

Junior wiggled all he could, but to no avail. Howard threw the rope over the arch and tied one end to his saddle horn. He then took the noose and put it over juniors head, and pulled it tight. He got on his horse and pulled the slake out of the rope until Junior had to stand when the rope got tighter.

Howard tied off the rope to the fence leaving Junior erect standing on the surrey. Howard said, "This is for the Bowies, Junior. You're going to meet your maker in a few minutes. I'll give you time to settle with him, before I hang you."

Howard waited a good while then said, "Goodbye, Junior and pulled the surrey away leaving Junior dangling. It was over, so Howard rode his horse over and removed all the ropes and gag. Junior was left with his hands beside him. He pulled the surrey over so it would look like Junior hung himself.

The moon was out and wasn't very bright. Howard lead his horse away about a hundred feet, then went back and with a piece of sage brush wiped out all his horse's hoof prints and his, just leaving the prints of surrey. He then walked away making sure he left no foot prints.

He went back to town and back to the saloon, and had a couple of more drinks. The bartender asked if he wanted another, but Howard said, "I'm too drunk, now." He then went to the hotel, and told the clerk he was too drunk to ride home. He got a room and went to sleep.

* * *

The next morning Bob Braxton got up, and as he generally did, went out on the front porch to finish his coffee. He sat looking at the sunrise then looked down toward the gate.

Something was hanging on the arch. He ran down there, which was only a hundred yards away, and there was Junior swaying in the breeze. Juniors eyes were nearly out of their sockets and his tongue was swollen and out of his mouth.

Bob just stood there for a moment looking at his only son. He said aloud, "I always knew your life would be short, Junior. I wonder if you hung yourself."

He dashed that thought. Junior was too selfish to do that. Bob looked around for prints, but only the surreys prints were there. That made him wonder if Junior really did take his own life.

He walked back to the bunkhouse and said, "Rowdy, take a couple of men and go to the front gate and cut Junior down. Someone hung him last night. Make as few prints as you can. Ruffins will want to investigate. Put Junior in the surrey and take him to Bill Owens. Tell Bill we'll be in tomorrow to bury him in town. Saddle my horse, I need to go to town."

CHAPTER 10

THE INVESTIGATION

Bob went to Ruffins home. He was eating breakfast. Ruffins asked, "What are you doing in town on Sunday, Bob?"

"Someone hung Junior last night on my front gate. It must have been Benson."

"No, it couldn't have been Benson. He and Lesley left on the stage for Springfield. They're on their honeymoon."

"They may have had horses down the road. I'm sure it was Benson."

"It could have been his partner, Howard Estep. He was in town for the wedding. I saw him heading for the saloon after the wedding."

Ruffins ate the last piece of toast, wiped his mouth on a napkin and got his hat. Bob followed him. The saloon was right around the corner and they walked. The saloon was closed, but they knocked on the door until Larken, the owner, came.

"You know I'm closed on Sunday, Ruffins. What's up?"

Larken then saw Bob and said, "Morning Bob."

Ruffins then said, "Someone hung Junior last night on Bob's gate. I'm here to ask about that guy with the tied down gun that's a partner of Benson. Do you know him?"

"Sure I know him. He was here after the wedding, and was here all evening. I saw him stumbling to the hotel. You may check there."

They left and went to the hotel. The clerk said, "Yeah, I know him. He came here about one this morning so drunk he could hardly walk. About an hour later, I could hear him snoring from down her. I went upstairs, and he'd left his door open. So I shut it. I came back downstairs, and could still hear him snoring. Most of my customers were drunk, so I didn't think he was bothering any of them. Did he cause problems at the saloon?"

"No, we were just checking his whereabouts. Did you see Benson and Lesley leave on the five o'clock stage for Springfield?"

"Me and everyone else in town. They were sure happy. I would be happy too, if I'd just married that Lesley."

"How far is the first way station going to Springfield, would you say?"

"About eighteen to twenty miles. That stage travels all night and the next day. Many people take it because it's the quickest way to Springfield."

"Let's ride, Ruffins. I want to make sure they went on to Springfield."

They mounted and left. Seven hours later they reached the way station. Ruffins asked about Benson and Lesley. "Yeah, they were here, that Lesley is a fine looking woman. They were both so happy, it made me happy. Why do you ask Sheriff?"

"I'm was just checking, Mort. Nothing to get excited about. Just routine you know."

They rode back to Ada and were worn out. Bob went to the hotel and Ruffins went home. Bob was lying in his bed and thought, *"If those two didn't do it, who would."* Then he thought, *"Nearly anyone. He surely wasn't liked. It could have been those three hands I fired. No… they seemed to like him. The rest of the crew were indifferent toward him. I guess that's a mystery that will never be solved. And really, what's the difference. I loved him, because he was my boy, but I surely didn't like him.*

* * *

Howard had his breakfast in town then rode out to the ranch. He took just enough time to make it look like he just discovered the ranch was burned. He rode back to town and got the sheriff. He was in his office. Sheriff Ruffins rode back with him. As they rode, he told Howard about Junior being hung.

Howard said, "Someone had a busy night. Do you suppose it was the same people who committed both crimes?"

"I don't know."

They found the bodies and the sheriff could tell that two had been shot, but the girl hadn't been.

He had Bill Owen come take what was left of them to town.

Bob woke at the hotel and the crew took Junior and buried him. Nothing was said. They just put him in the grave and covered it up. As they were shoveling the dirt, Bob thought, *"I'll bet Benson paid someone to hang Junior. That's it, he paid to have it done. Well, two can play that game."*

* * *

The honeymoon was great. Lesley said, "I don't know why people pay so much money to go away for a honeymoon. All you want to do is hold one another."

"Well, you got me through it okay. I'm pretty dumb when it comes to women."

"You did alright for a novice, Thomas. You couldn't have been better had you been experienced. I'm so in love with you."

They stayed a week then returned. As they were getting out of the stage, Howard was there with a grime look on his face. He said, "I have some bad news, Thomas. Someone came and killed all the Bowies and burned all the structures on the ranch. I was in town having some drinks and got so drunk, I spent the night in the hotel. I found them the next morning."

Thomas didn't say anything for a moment then he smiled and said, "Do you remember the look on Ed's face when he saw Skillet in Texas?"

"Howard said, "Yes, that memory will be with me tell I die. I think of it now and again. They were sure nice people. They surely didn't deserve what they got."

"I don't know, they loved the Lord so much you could almost feel the presence of the Lord when Ed prayed."

"Lesley said, "You two really loved them. Few people have people who love them that much. I'm fortunate to have two men who love me."

Thomas said, "There's no reason to go back to the ranch today. We'll need to start rebuilding the house soon. I'm going to hire a builder to build us a splendid home, Lesley."

"What about the store, Thomas?"

"We can do that too, if you want."

"I haven't thought that much about it while we were gone, but now we have to make the decision.

* * *

Bob decided to go to St. Louis to find someone to kill Benson. He had heard of the James brothers and the Younger brothers. They were from Liberty, not far from St. Louis. He was sure he could find someone there.

He told Rowdy he needed to be away for awhile, and not to tell anyone. Rowdy said, "I can run things okay. Take your time. I'll just need you to give me enough cash to pay the men."

"I have plenty of money in the safe for that. I'll give you the combination."

"Gosh Boss, that's a lot of responsibility. Do you think I can handle it?"

"Sure, Rowdy. Now that Junior's gone, you'll have to take a bigger role. If something happens to me, I've left a will with Brooks, the banker. You will have to carry out my wishes,

Rowdy. I'm giving you a thirty dollar raise, but having to run this place, you'll earn every cent of it. I want you to live in the house, now. You can take Junior's bedroom. Clean out all his stuff. I don't want to be reminded of him when I return. I loved him dearly, but I didn't like him. God knew what he was doing when he took Junior. He caused everyone around him grief. I'm leaving at first light. Just tell the boys I needed to get away."

* * *

In St. Louis, he found a man who knew Cole Younger. He said, "I'll give you ten dollars if you'll get Cole to meet with me."

The man said, "I'll see what I can do."

Three days later there was a knock at his door. A tall man with a tied down gun was standing there. He said, "I'm Cole Younger. You wanted to see me?"

"Yes, I have a favor to ask of you. Won't you come in?"

Younger didn't immediately come in. He stuck his head in and looked around then stepped through the door.

Bob said, "Have a seat over there, would you have a drink?"

"No, I'm here on business. What do you want?"

"I want you to kill a man for me. I'll give you five hundred dollars if you'll do it."

"What did he do to you?"

"He hung my only son."

"I guess that's a good enough reason."

"What did your son do to him?"

"He slapped his girlfriend."

"Yeah, some men are touchy that way. Me, I try not to get that close to women. I just use the saloon girls. You generally don't get that attached to a whore.

"I'll do the job for you. How do you want it done?"

"I want him killed by a high powered rifle from distance. That way no one would ever know who did it. I will give you three hundred now and send you two hundred after it's done. You know I'll pay you. I don't want that high powered rifle shooting me."

Cole laughed and said, "Yes, I know you'll pay me."

"How will I know who he is?"

"He's building a ranch house just west of town about two miles out. Here, I brought a map to show you. I'll try to get a picture of him. Do you have someplace for me to send it?"

"Yes. Send it to Ron Edwards, general delivery, Liberty, Missouri. I don't want to dally on this, as I have other things to do. I'll expect the picture next week."

While in St. Louis, Bob engaged a photographer. He said, "I want to surprise my brother with a photo of his son for this birthday. His son lives in Ada, Missouri and is building a house, just west of town about two miles. I don't want anyone to know you're doing this, so you must be secretive about your work. When you have the photo send it to Ron Edwards, general delivery, Liberty, Missouri. Here's fifty-dollars now, and I'll send you another fifty when Ron gets the picture. Is that okay?"

"You've got the right man, Mister."

Two weeks later Cole had the picture and had found him a place that overlooked the building site. He had a scope on his rifle and knew just where Benson would be. He zeroed in on that spot and knew that the next day he would kill him. He had his horse tied in a strategic spot for a perfect getaway.

The next day Lesley was with Benson. Cole had his spot, but didn't see Lesley as she was bent over tying her shoe. Just as she raised up, Cole shot and it hit her in the head and deflected the bullet enough so when it immerged, it didn't hit Thomas.

Lesley fell into Thomas arms and he knew she was dead. He looked to where the shot had come from and went that direction. He found where a horse had been tied and then an empty cartridge from a Sharps fifty caliber. He went back and picked up Lesley. The workers were all gathered around and work stopped.

Thomas drove her into town. Howard was in town picking up building material. He saw Thomas driving into town in his buggy with Lesley draped over him. He ran as fast as he could and saw her. Half her head was blown away. It was a gross sight.

He said, "What happened, Thomas?"

"Someone with a high powered rifle shot her. I think they were firing at me. Lesley was bent over to tie her shoe, and just as the shot came, she raised up and caught it in the head."

Howard said, "Braxton! He had this done."

"Not so loud. We'll handle this together. First let's get Lesley into Bill's place. We'll want to put her in the ground tomorrow as the weather is rather warm."

That afternoon they sat at their hotel room. Thomas said, "We'll handle this like you handled Junior."

"How do you know I hung Junior?"

Thomas smiled and said, "I know you, Howard. When

you saw the Bowie family burned up, you tracked down Junior that night, and hung him. You then went back to the saloon where you had been earlier, and continued to drink the rest of the evening. You never talk to anyone, so no one knew you were gone. Larken said you were there all evening. But I know you as well as I know myself. You did the right thing. I bet you enjoyed it."

"Yes, Junior was conscious the whole time, and knew just what was going to happen. He peed his pants when I had him standing there. I gave him a few minutes to talk to Jesus, then hung him. I swore, I'd never tell you."

"The sheriff's final ruling was that Junior committed suicide. He spent a lot of time investigating. I think Braxton thought I had hired it done. That's how he got the idea of having someone kill me. Just to keep him from hiring someone else, we need to tend to him before too long.

"Well, we have another hanging to plan. Let's wait until the house and barn are built. Let's let him think he's safe. I don't care who he hired. It was Braxton who pulled the trigger in my mind. Where do you think we should hang him. His ranch is too far out and no one would see him, but his ranch hands."

"There's a big oak tree with high limbs at the church. The church is visible from nearly every angle of town, as it sits higher than the buildings in town. We could hang him Saturday night so all the church crowd will see him the next morning."

"That's a good idea, the church it is. I think Braxton will keep a low profile now. I hear he left town about six weeks ago. They say he was mourning Junior. Heck, I think you did him a favor. He ought to have sent money to us, instead of hiring a killer."

Braxton now went no where without two or three of his men with him. He did go into town on Saturday night. He stayed at the hotel, as he now attended church on Sunday. He wanted to look respectable. He needed friends now that Junior was gone.

Thomas and Howard were talking one evening. Now that the barn was finished, they were staying out at their place.

Thomas said, "Where do you want to go, Howard. With all the sadness around here, I surely don't want to stay in Ada. We'll start selling the livestock off gradually. We'll have Anderson sell the ranch. More people are coming in, and we should make a profit.

"Why do you say 'we'. You own the ranch and I work for you. I like it that way."

"No, now that Lesley's gone, I've moved you up to partner. You didn't answer my question. Where do you want to go?"

"How about Texas. We really didn't get to see much of it. We were just in and out."

"Sounds good to me. Texas is a big state. Lets go down there and mosey around some. We might find some place we like."

The house was completed, but they didn't move in. They thought it would bring a higher price if it were new.

Anderson had it on the market and several people wanted it. They set a price of ten thousand dollars on it. Anderson said, "You'll never get that. No one has that kind of money."

"Try to sell it to Braxton. He has that kind of money. He offered Rush two thousand. I just want you to tell us what he says, and how he looks, when you tell him the price."

Anderson laughed and said, "I'll do that. It will be worth my time just to see his face."

When Braxton came in on Saturday night he always had the same room. He made a deal to rent it every Saturday night all year long.

Anderson called on him. He said, "I remember you wanted to buy the ole Rush place, now the Benson place. Benson wants to sell out. I think since Lesley is gone, he wants to settle in another part of the country."

"Yes, I always wanted that place. I understand that he built a nice house on it."

"Yes, I've seen it. He never moved in because he wanted the next owner to have a brand new place. It has a huge barn now and is new like the house."

"What does he want for it?"

"He says it's a premium place and should have a premium price. He wants ten thousand dollars."

Ten thousand dollars! Is he nuts?"

"No, he'll probably get it. It's close to town, so women folk can shop easily and has nearly a section of land that doesn't need fencing. He has a numbers pastures to move the stock around, and enough tillable land to plant enough feed to last the winter. It's an ideal place. If one is going to have a woman, he'll want her close to town, I think it's worth it. I have advised him to hold out for his price.

"What do you care what it cost, Bob. Now that Junior's gone, you owe it to yourself. You might even catch a good looking widow to take care of you in your old age."

"Well, that is something to think about. I need a woman now that Junior's gone. He was a lot of company, but I knew

I could never have a wife with him around. I think that is partially why Janie ran off. You've got me thinking, Herb. I don't have anyone to leave my money to, and I'm getting up in age. I think you're right. Tell him I'll buy it. No, don't. Tell him someone out of town is buying it, and you can't disclose the name at this time."

"Yes, I can see what you mean, but I know he don't hold any grudges against you and told me so. All his hard feelings were for Junior. But, even he thought Junior's hanging was a terrible thing. He told me that he really believes that Junior took his own life. He said that all the misery he caused you, and then Lesley turning him down, did him in. He was really remorseful about Junior."

After Herb left, he went directly to his house where Thomas and Howard were waiting. Thomas said, "I bet he cursed when you told him the price."

"I was astounded Thomas, I think he's going to buy it. He didn't know how you would feel about selling it to him, so I had to do a bit of lying.

"I told him you were remorseful over Junior's death. I said you thought Junior took his own life, because of the misery he caused you, and then Lesley turning him down. He bought it, and now I think he's going to give you ten thousand. I would never have believed it."

Howard said, "You could sell ice boxes to Eskimos, Herb. You're certainly in the right business. With a tongue like yours, you could probably talk a good looking widow into marrying you."

"You know I've started thinking that way. With Lesley

gone, I get lonesome, and now you two are leaving. I think I'll start looking around."

That night, they were lying on their cots and Thomas said, "You know I've been thinking about Braxton. I know he took Lesley's life, but unintentionally. Hanging him won't bring Lesley back. It will be just one more murder that I have to think about. What say we forget that, and just move on."

"You know, I was thinking along those lines myself, Thomas. Hanging Junior had to be done, but Braxton's different. He helps people, and is now going to church every Sunday. I agree, let's just drift."

They sold the house to Braxton. Thomas was alone with him and said, "I didn't have anything to do with hanging your son. I know you tried to have me killed, but then Lesley raised up just as he shot. I really believe that Junior took his own life.

"I was thinking about killing you before I left, but that wouldn't bring Lesley back. I really hope you find someone to love you. You ruined Juniors life and he ruined yours, so I guess that's even now. You needn't ever fear that I will take revenge. I killed sixty-seven men during the war. Some of them were just boys. I don't want to have one more person's death on my conscious. The Lord forgave me for those killings as it was war. Killing people now would be murder, and I will try my best not break the Lord's commandment again. Have a good life, Braxton. We're leaving tomorrow. You'll find we left you the chickens and a couple of cows to milk."

Thomas got up and to his surprise, Braxton had tear in his eyes. He said, "I wish you had been my son, Thomas, you're everything a father would be proud of."

CHAPTER 11

DALLAS

They took Thomas' buggy, but tied Howard's horse behind. They both had their saddles and enough grub to last a week or so. They had a map and were headed for Ft. Worth. From there, they had no idea where they may go. They thought they would talk to several people about different parts of Texas.

They reached Tulsa and drove due south. Instead of reaching Ft. Worth they came to a town called Dallas. It was nearly as big as St. Louis. They were both surprised. There were several hotels and the downtown was enormous. They asked a man standing on a corner where the best hotel in Dallas was.

The man pointed to a hotel down the street that appeared much larger than the building's around it. He said, "It's called the Grand Hotel, and for a reason. It's the grandest structure in the city of Dallas."

Thomas said, "Thank you, and they drove to the hotel. As they drove up, a man in a uniform asked if they would be staying at the hotel.

Thomas said, "Yes, we will, if they have a room for us."

"There'll be room enough. I'll take your horses and buggy after we remove your luggage. We have a stable and a place to store your buggy. It's part of the service."

By that time there were several men in uniforms that surrounded them and helped them with there bags. As they were walking to the counter, Thomas said, "Let's live big for a little while, Howard. Lord knows, we will have some thin livin' soon enough."

"Well it's your dime, Thomas, spend it like you want."

They arrived at the counter and the clerk asked, "How may I help you."

Thomas said, "Do you have a suite with two bedrooms?"

The clerk grinned and said, "I have just the suite for you, Sir. It faces the mezzanine, so you will be close to our dining facilities and the street, should you like to shop. We get four dollars a day for it."

"We'll take it for five days," and laid down a double eagle.

The clerk smiled and said, "I'll see that your luggage and saddles are put away neatly, Sir. Here's your keys," and handed both a key.

Thomas signed the register then asked, "We need to buy some clothes. Is there a department store close?"

"Yes Sir, there is. Just down the street, you'll find the largest department store in Texas. You can find fine clothes there. They have tailoring also, just ask for Mr. Meeker and say that Travis sent you. That will get you the help you need."

Howard said, "Why do we need new clothes, Thomas?"

Because when we go to dinner tonight I want to look like people who dine in New York City, however, with a western touch."

"Like I say, it's your dime."

The suits they bought were splendid. They were made of the best material and had a western touch. They were tailored to fit them marvelously. They also bought new boots and Stetson hats. Howard couldn't believe the price, but Thomas said, "Braxton is paying for this," and Howard laughed.

They had a hot bath, a shave and a haircut. They put on their new suits and walked downstairs to the dining room. The headwaiter had been notified that these were prime customers and they were surprised when he said, "Right this way, Mr. Benson."

Howard turned his way and said, "You're already casting a large shadow here in Dallas."

They were seated in a prime place. Just as they were being seated, a man rose from the next table and said, "My lord! It's my prize medical student, Thomas Benson."

Thomas turned and there stood Dr. Phillips from the Mt. Sinai School of Medicine."

Thomas smiled and said, "It's good to see you, Dr. Phillips."

As they were shaking hands the other man stood and said, "Do you remember me, Thomas?"

"Dr. Bernstein. I would never forget you." Thomas then turned and said, "Let me introduce my partner, Howard Estep."

Bernstein said, "I'm pleased to know you Dr. Estep."

Howard grinned and said, "I'm no doctor, Sir, just a man who served with Major Benson."

"Oh yes. Your father told us about your service, Thomas. We were surprised to learn you were a cavalry officer instead of a medical doctor.

"Please let me introduce my nieces, Lila and Callie. Both men turned and saw two beautiful women who looked just alike, as they were twins Both put out their hands. Thomas and Howard took their hands and bowed.

Dr. Phillips turned to the head waiter and said, "Please put our tables together. This man was as close to me as a son. He was lost and now he's found. I want to rejoice. After you have put our tables together, bring us two bottles of your finest champagne. This is a night to celebrate."

After they were all seated Thomas asked, "Why are you in Dallas, Dr. Phillips?"

"We have been requested, by the state of Texas, to start a medical school in Dallas. My two nieces have just graduated from nurses training and asked to come with us. When we arrived I sought a land man to find a proper location for the medical school. After that was settled I told him we would need someplace to live that was close to the medical school. To our incredible luck, he showed us a place right across the street. It's a mansion. It was built just before the war started. It was two years in the construction. The man building it never moved in. As he was from New York, he moved back immediately after Ft. Sumner was fired upon.

"It was boarded up during the war as no one wanted to pay the price for it, when a war was being fought. It has ten bedrooms all with their own water closets and fireplaces. You'll see it, as I want you to stay with us. I have so much to talk about with you. Please say you'll stay with us."

"Of course. We have a lot to catch up on."

"Well, I don't want to get into the medical school conversation tonight, but tomorrow I want to talk at length about it."

Dr. Bernstein said, "That's all we talk about since agreeing to start a school."

The champagne arrived and they toasted. Dr. Bernstein said, "To the smartest medical student I ever taught."

Thomas said, "Come Dr. Bernstein, that can't be true."

Phillips said, "It is. We discussed it several times. You not only had a mind with great ingenuity, but the hands of a skilled surgeon.

"Well, let me toast to two dear friends, and I say that from the bottom of my heart."

Howard said, "I would like to toast the beautiful women you brought, Dr. Phillips."

Dr. Phillips said, "I see Howard has an eye of for beauty."

Thomas said, "I don't think he has ever been out with a woman, but he does have a fine eye."

Lila said, "You're making me blush, Mr. Estep."

Callie said, "What a lie, Lila, you haven't blushed since you were twelve years old," and they all laughed.

It was a delightful party and a delightful meal."

When they were in their rooms that night, Howard said, "You know they are going to rope you into helping them with that medical school don't you."

"Sure."

"If they do what will I do?"

"Enter medical school of course. You will be their first student."

"Me a doctor?"

"Yes, you have to make up for all the people you killed during the war, Howard."

"That does put a different perspective to it. I think you're right." He then said, "I could just see my dad's face if I told him I was a doctor. He'd say, 'bullshit,'" and they both laughed.

The next morning as they were going to breakfast, Thomas stopped by the front desk and said, "I have been invited to stay with Dr. Phillips and will not require the hotel's services."

The clerk said, "My, I have heard of Dr. Phillips. He bought the Barbour mansion. You are in high company, Mr. Benson. I will return your sixteen dollars."

"Take a couple of dollars for yourself. You have been more than kind."

The clerk smiled and said, "You are generous, Mr. Benson. I will distribute your tip with the bellboys. Thank you again."

After breakfast they had the bellboys help them take their things down and load them on their buggy. They drove to the mansion as Dr. Phillips had told them the route.

When they were about a block from the mansion, Howard said, "My lord, look at that thing."

The mansion stood in the middle of four acres that had been landscaped marvelously. It sat on a low hill that put it about all the structures around it. It had a low stone wall as not to obscure the beautiful landscaping around it. Statues were on all corners for the wall and the entrances. It sat back from the street and had a circular driveway made of decretive bricks that had a pattern within it. It went under a veranda that the driveway went under. The veranda was supported with marble columns that gave it a regal look.

Behind the mansion were several buildings that included a carriage house and barn. These structures were built to resemble the architecture of the mansion.

They pulled up in front of the mansion and an attendant helped them unload their things. Then another attendant drove the buggy away.

They were met by the two doctors who had coffee waiting for them in a sitting room off the great room. The great room was over forty feet in height. Looking from the front door you could see a marble stairway that split halfway up to the second floor. It then went up to the third floor.

In the drawing room sat the two women dressed in beautiful dresses. One in yellow and the other orange. Both Thomas' and Howard's eyes went directly to them. The women both stood and came to them with their hand outstretched.

After addressing everyone and being seated, Dr. Phillips said, "You know we want you to help us establish the medical school don't you, Thomas?"

"Yes, I surmised you would ask me."

"We sent a letter this morning telling the New York City Medical School to send you a diploma. We know it will be granted, because both Dr. Bernstein and I along with Dr. Martin and Dr. Tilden, are on the board.

"We all will have to apply for a medical license with the state of Texas, but that is merely a formality. Dr. Bernstein and I have structured a program for the medical school, but we want you to read it over carefully and give us your comments."

"We have also thought of your colleague, Mr. Estep. We want you to be our first student. You told us you had a college degree and we are hoping you will accept our offer."

Thomas laughed and said, "We were just discussing that this morning and Howard is willing. He did say you would be taking on a project."

Callie said, "We were discussing that subject after we heard the doctors talking and both agreed to help him closely with his studies," and the all laughed.

That afternoon Dr. Phillips and Thomas were walking in the garden and Thomas said, "When we were talking this morning at breakfast about Howard becoming a doctor. We talked about all the killing we had done during the war, and thought if we could save the same amount of sick people, it may make up for the killing we did.

"Killing is a hard thing. You don't just kill the man, but you strike a terrible blow on his mother and father, plus his brothers and sisters. In some cases his wife and children. I tried not to look on the men I faced as people, but rather just the enemy.

"I knew what I was doing was terrible, but I was good at it. I thought of transferring to the medical corps, but I was needed in the cavalry. I was much better at that then removing legs and arms.

"I thought I could end the war sooner, and that would save a lot of lives. I tried not to keep count of the number of men I killed, but it was impossible as each one of them were indelible. I now hope I can double that number in lives saved."

"It was a terrible thing for you, Thomas, but it had a purpose. I never question God and his plan. The war came for a reason. I think it brought many people to accept our Lord Jesus."

"I know it did. I did work removing bullets and sowing up

wounds on my own battalion. Many men called me doctor rather than major. I did this throughout the war, so I was practicing medicine all through the war between battles."

"I also prayed with many men who were dying or near death's door. It brought me closer to the Lord.

"Howard was a mighty warrior. I was not a friend of his during the war, as I made no friends and had none. You can't make friends, then send them to their death. I sent many of my men to their death, so I didn't want to know anyone on a personal basis.

"However, I ran into Howard in Joplin, Missouri. He was as glad to see me as I was he. Fighting side by side built a bond between us. We shall never part again.

"You know I was married after the war. She knew Howard and she said a strange thing to me. She said, I love you with all my heart. I just hope I can love you as much as Howard loves you."

"Later, it brought tears to my eyes."

"What happened to your wife, Thomas."

"She took a bullet meant for me."

"Rather than hunt down the guy, we decided that we had done enough killing. Howard and I decided to sell out, and head for Texas. We ended up here in Dallas where you saw us.

"This is a great challenge, Thomas. We will have a hospital to run along with the medical school. We will have several doctors coming when we get the hospital up and running.

* * *

The hospital was now built and the medical school started.

Howard was doing well with his studies and like Callie had said, She was helping him with his studies. It wasn't six months until they decided to marry.

Lila and Thomas weren't that enamored with one another. Lila could see that Thomas was more involved with his work than with his interest in her. She wanted a man solely devoted to her. She found that in a young doctor by the name of Farley Ward.

Farley was a handsome man and fell madly in love with Lila. Lila moved out of the mansion after they were wed, and into a house that Farley had bought.

Dr. Phillips was talking to Thomas after the wedding and said, "I thought you and Lila would marry someday."

"No, I haven't gotten over my first wife. I wish you could have known her. We really loved each other. I don't know if I will ever marry again."

"Yes, I know what you mean. After Marylyn died, I didn't want another. I went out a few times with women a year or so after she passed, but none of them were even close to what Marylyn was. I finally just gave it up."

CHAPTER 12

MARY LOGAN

Two years went by and the medical school and hospital were doing well. Howard was doing quite well in his classes and both he and Callie were happy. They had a little boy that year, and named him Thomas.

Thomas was deeply involved with his work at the medical school and the hospital. He was the chief surgeon now. He constantly read about new procedures that were developing around the medical world. He even left several times to study and watch new surgery methods that were used around the country.

He went back to New York City several times and looked in on his old friends while watching something new in the medical field.

Two doctors were hired by Dr. Phillips to work at the

hospital. They were married. It was the first woman doctor that many had ever seen. She was popular and beautiful. Their names were Fred and Mary Logan.

Fred was an internal medicine doctor and Mary was a surgeon. Thomas was with her everyday for several hours. She wanted to assist Thomas on every surgery. They spent hours talking about each procedure before they operated. Plastic surgery was now being talked about. Many soldiers had been disfigured during the war.

Mary was interested in plastic surgery, also. Both read everything they could find on the subject. It was quite popular in Europe. Thomas decided to see some skin grafting that was being done in Paris. He talked to Dr. Phillips and Bernstein about it and they encouraged him to go.

When Mary found he was going, she asked to go along. She had first talked with her husband about it, and he agreed she should go. Mary was fond of Thomas though he never noticed. She had lost interest with Fred and he with her. They now slept in separate bedrooms. She said it was because of his snoring, but really she didn't want to bed him anymore. He was crude and selfish in that area.

Thomas loved to talk to her about plastic surgery. He said, "I've seen many soldiers who are so disfigured that they are shunned socially. Just think what we could do if we were able to correct much of that and make them whole again."

"This is what Mary loved about Thomas. She dreamed about being with him in the bedroom as well as at the operating table. She couldn't take her eyes off of him. Thomas was so into the work he never noticed. He never thought about her as a woman. After all she was married. That made her asexual as far as he was concerned.

They were in New York and he took her to a restaurant that he particularly liked. It served French cuisine with sauces that were beyond delicious. After the meal, they listen to a small band that played soft music that was popular at the time.

When they reached their rooms. Mary said, "Would you give me a hug before we retire. A woman needs a hug now and then."

Thomas thought nothing about it until he was in her arms. She held him tightly and put her cheek to his neck and held him much longer than a normal hug. After they stepped back, she looked at him and said, "Don't you feel something for me, Thomas?"

He was speechless, because he did. He finally said, "Yes, and that is a problem. I believe in the sanctity of marriage. I think of Fred and what he would feel."

"Our marriage has been over for over a year. We sleep in separate bedrooms. Our marriage is just a habit rather that a love nest. Why don't you come in and we'll talk about it."

Thomas thought again and said, "Let's talk about it in the morning when we are totally sober. We had too much wine tonight and that brings on lust. Do I make sense?"

"You always make sense, but sometimes you have to let love lead the way, wine or no wine."

"We want each other now, but we may be very sorry in the morning. Let's sleep on it and approach this logically." With that said, he whirled around and opened his door and went in. He had his back to the door now, and knew he had done the right thing.

He could still feel her hot breath on his neck and feel her warm body meshed to his. He had never looked at her in that way, but now he wanted her the worst way. He knew it wasn't right, but he wanted her.

The next morning at breakfast, neither said a thing. They ate in silence. Finally Thomas said, "Aren't you glad now that we didn't give into our lust?"

Mary said, "No. Like I said, my marriage is over. I think I'll file for divorce when we return."

"Now think of how that would look. We go to Paris for six weeks and the minute you return you file for divorce."

"You're right. I can't do that. But what can we do, I love you. I have loved you for a long time. It's not just the lust from last night. I love you in the operating room, and in the clinic where we discuss every operation. I long for you at night. I know it isn't right, but there it is.

"As I look back, I began to dislike Fred when I started working with you. You are everything he isn't. Your dedication, your warmth with patients and the way you treat everyone. My love wasn't instantaneous, it grew bit by bit until I was saturated with it."

"To be as candid as I can, I never looked at you as a woman. You were just a doctor to me. I loved your work and time with you, but like I said, you were just a doctor and not a woman. Last night when you held me so tightly, I began to want you. I saw you as a woman I wanted to be with. All the things I liked about you came to a point, as a woman I wanted to hold. It can't be, Mary. There are some things in life that we just can't have, and that's each other.

"Let's not ruin our trip to Paris with this. We are both

dedicated doctors. There are so many people out there who need our skill, badly. Will we deny them that, because we want to sleep with one another. I think of how it was during the war. Each battle I knew I would probably be killed, but so many soldiers depended on me, I think God protected me and kept me alive. I thought of them and my fear of dying quelled.

"I know I love you, but those same soldiers are now crying out to both of us to save them. What are we to do?"

"I guess that's why I love you so much Thomas. You have such a love for your fellow man. It is so Christ like. I wish I could love Jesus so much that the thought of holding you would go away. I think that is what it will be like when we are with Jesus. There will be no sexual love, because He will give us a love that supersede sexual love, and we will not need it. But, for now it's hard. However, you have made me see that the love for those that need our skills, supersedes my selfish love. I will do what you say. We will put away our lust and do the right thing."

Thomas picked up her hand and said, "I love you, Mary."

"She said, "And I love you Thomas."

They went to Paris and stayed eight weeks. They even were asked to do some skin grafts themselves.

When they returned they addressed the medical staff. Mary said, "We stayed two weeks longer than we were supposed to, but we really needed to stay a year or more. There are procedures going on in Brussels, Berlin and Burn that we ought to see. I watched Doctor Benson some, and I have never seen such satisfaction on a face. I think we can do the things they are doing in Europe here, but we need more knowledge."

Thomas then talked. He said, "There are still hundreds if not thousands of soldiers that were disfigured during the war. We need to help those men. They need a new start in life. If Dr. Phillips will give me the funding, I am going back to Europe to study for a year. I think I should go alone. I can teach Dr. Logan the procedures when I return."

Dr. Fred Logan said, "If you are just doing this for me, Dr. Benson, I will gladly go without Mary for a year to help those men. I would go myself if I had your's and Mary's skill, so please take her."

Thomas was stuck. He thought he was home free, but now Fred had made it impossible.

Thomas decided to talk to Dr. Phillips about it. He told every detail he could remember.

Dr. Phillips was quiet for a long time then he said, "You are the finest man I ever knew. I knew I loved you, but nothing like I love you now. You are as near to being like Christ of any man I know. I know you love her, and she loves you, but you see mankind as above that.

"I see why you tried to dodge being with Mary for a year. As beautiful as Mary is, I don't think any man on earth could be with her and not bend. I'll see that she doesn't go. I'll make it look like a budgetary thing."

The next staff meeting Dr. Phillips went over the budget. He even had it put on a blackboard. He showed where they only had funds for Dr. Benson to go for a year.

A day later, Mary asked Dr. Phillips if she could talk to him. He thought, *"She is going to try and talk me into letting her go using her own funds."*

When they were alone, Mary said, "Thomas talked to you and told you everything didn't he?"

Dr. Phillips said, "Thomas is like my own son, Mary. He told me everything in such detail I could feel your love. He loves you dearly, but he loves those disfigured soldiers who gave more than their lives. He is more like Christ then any man I know. Don't break him, Mary. Let him help those soldiers. He can teach you when he returns. If you go, you will break that bond. No man who knows you love them, could keep from loving you."

"She was crying now. She said, "I'm glad Thomas has you Dr. Phillips. You must be my father, too. I will say I will leave Fred while he's gone. I don't want to live with him anymore, and I think he feels the same. We will be friends as we were before we married. I need to live alone awhile. I think I will be a better doctor if I do. I will dedicate myself. Probably not as much as Thomas, but I will try."

Before Thomas went, he talked to Howard. They still found time everyday to talk as they were dedicated to each other.

Thomas said, "I want you to be a plastic surgeon, Howard. We will work together."

"That's my dream, Thomas. But just think what we could have done if we stayed in Ada. We may be running over a hundred head now," they both laughed.

Thomas said, "I wonder how many people go by and put flowers on Juniors grave," and they laughed again. He then said, "You know what I miss most about Lesley? It was her laugh. I can still hear her laugh. I still miss her terribly."

"You must. If I spent eight weeks with that Mary I would be in love for sure. That woman's a looker."

"But married, Howard."

"Thomas, you're twice the man I'll ever be. I think that is why Christ put me with you. He knew I was too weak to stand alone. I still think of you in battle. Everyman looked at you for leadership and you gave it to them. I wish Sergeant Rimes would have lived. I bet he would be right here with us. Talk about someone devoted to you, he was rapt.

"Well, I'll miss you, Thomas, but I see you have a higher calling. Had I been you, I would have come out of my own pocket to finance Mary's trip. But that sure isn't you."

"You know what keeps me a straight arrow, Howard? People expect it of me."

Howard thought a minute and said, "Man, you're deep, Thomas."

Thomas mapped out his trip before he left. Every place in Europe that had plastic surgery invited him. He went to Brussels first.

He had picked up some French while he was in Paris. But in Brussels he hired a tutor and became fairly literate in French. He now spoke only French. Most people he dealt with spoke several languages.

In Brussels he saw the doctors rebuild a face. It took several operations and he knew the patient went through tremendous pain. He told one patient, "I don't know who has the harder job. The surgeon who worked on you, or the pain you had to endure."

The patient said, "If you looked like me, you could endure anything. I want my life back again."

While in Brussels he received a letter from Mary. She said,

"I hope you are missing me as much as I am missing you. I pretend my pillow is you at night."

He was in Brussels a half year. He then went to Berlin. He could tell almost immediately that they were far ahead of the doctors in Brussels. He stayed the rest of his time there. He was even invited to do some of the procedures.

He received no more letters from Mary. He thought, *"Just as well, all it does is make me want her."*

He returned and they began practicing the procedures he had learned. Howard was at every operation as was Mary. The three talked every procedure over in depth before that touched a scalpel to skin. Even though Howard hadn't graduated yet, he was at every session that he could make.

Thomas was still asked at times to do operation that were very difficult. Everyone knew he had the most skill of anyone.

He had been home for over a year when Mary said, "Why don't you take me to dinner tonight. We can have Howard and Callie go with us. I don't think tongues would wag as we are all together everyday. Even Callie is working, now that her mother has come to Dallas."

Thomas agreed. While they were eating and laughing Thomas thought this is how it should be. *"I wish the four of us could be together every evening."*

Dr. Phillips received a wire from Paris. It asked if he would send Doctor Benson to Paris. They had a new procedure and felt he should be there. Dr. Phillips read the wire to Thomas in the presents of Mary and Howard.

Thomas left the next day. He caught an ocean liner out of Galveston.

CHAPTER 13

THE SHEIK AND PARIS

The ship stopped in the Bermuda Islands to pick up more passengers. They traveled on to the Canary Island where a group of Arabs boarded the ship. When they were once more at sea, the captain sent Thomas a message that said he wanted to see him in his cabin. Thomas went immediately. When he entered there were several Arabs there all dressed in robes.

The captain said, "Let me introduce you to Aga Kahn. He is an emir in Jerusalem he wants you to go with him there to perform an operation on one of his sons. The son has a birth defect of the face that he feels you can correct. He has tried to get one of the doctors from Paris, Berlin and Brussels, but they turned him down. He says he is prepared to pay you ten thousand America dollars, and see that you are retuned to Paris immediately after the operation."

Please tell the emir that I am humbled that he has asked me, but I do not have the skills at this point in time, as I am still learning. He must seek some skilled surgeon in Paris. I wish I could help, but cannot."

His words were translated to the emir and the emir nodded and left with his people. Thomas left and thought nothing of it again.

They docked in Morocco and were going to be there just one day, and then travel on. That would leave him time to see the city, so he engaged a guide who spoke English. He was taken to a Moroccan bar where he was served a tasting drink. That was all he remembered until he awoke in a cabin aboard a ship. There were two men in his room who he immediately gathered were guards. They were dressed in robes so he surmised he had been kidnapped, by the emir.

They fed his meals in his cabin. None of the men who guarded him spoke to him. They talked to each other in Arabic, but then not too much. He had no idea where he was, or where he was being taken. They were at sea four days then came to a port. He was taken off the ship and put in a hotel. He was allowed a bath and a change of clothes. The clothes were robes like the Arabs wore. The next morning he was taken in a coach going east. There were two men in the coach and a woman. She spoke English and said, "You are being taken to Jerusalem. We will be there tonight. You will have a day's rest then the next day you will see your patient. Two doctors will assist you. They both speak English as they were educated in London, where they went through medical school.

"Any questions?"

"What will I be required to do?"

"I do not know that. The doctors who will assist you will be able to answer all your medical questions."

Thomas then knew he would be working on the boy that the emir had requested. That night they reached Jerusalem. He was taken to some nice quarters. It had a bathroom with a tub. He found soap and towels. The tub was filled with warm water, so he undressed and got in. A woman appeared and began to wash him. He didn't say anything, and let her wash him. He got out of the tub and she gave him a towel, and he dressed.

Dinner was brought in and placed on a table that had a linen table cloth. Nice china and silverware were place there. Soon a cart was brought in and steaming hot food placed on the table. The woman sat down and so did Thomas, and they ate. Not a word passed between them. A boy stood by while they ate, and when they were through, he took their used dishes on a tray and removed them.

Thomas said nothing. The lady turned down the lamps, so Thomas put on a nightshirt that was on the bed and got into bed. The woman removed all her clothes and got in beside him. Thomas rolled over with his back to the woman and went to sleep.

When he awoke the woman was gone. However, a man appeared shortly with his American clothes that had been cleaned and pressed. His luggage was there, also. He dressed and went with the man. They went in a carriage for about a mile, then went into a place that appeared to be a hospital.

He was taken to a place where two men stood. One of them said, "I am Dr. Shaed and this is Dr. Dorma. Our patient is in the next room. We know how to operate on the boys face, but we will need you to take skin from his leg and graft it to boy's face. We are not skilled at this, and it must be done perfect."

They then went into the next room and the boy was lying on an operating table. Thomas could picture the procedure in his mind. He said, "I see what you are doing and I can do my part just after you finish. Is there any anesthesia?"

Dr. Dorma said, "Yes, and I will administer it. The doctor then started the anesthesia. A few moments later Dr. Shaed began the operation. He was skilled and finished in less than an hour.

Thomas then measured the wound he would cover, and then marked it on the boy's leg where he wanted to remove the skin. Expertly, he removed the skin and sewed it onto the boy. His work took just under two hours as he was very careful making intricate sutures which were many.

When he was through, Dr. Shaed said, "That was remarkable. I must learn that procedure. You are very skilled."

"Will I be permitted to leave now?"

"No, but if there is no redness or swelling, you will be permitted to go in about six day."

While he was waiting, he requested and was granted a tour of Jerusalem. He got to see the temple mount and places around it. He thought to himself, *"This was worth it. I would never have been able to see this if I hadn't been abducted."*

What they told him proved to be true, and six days later after he had visited the boy. He was amazed at the transformation of the boy from a terrible face to one that was pleasing in looks.

As he was traveling, he thought, *"I'm not going to report this as had I known the whole story I would have done it."*

When he was put on a ship he asked where he was heading and was told, "Morocco." He went to his cabin to put his clothes away and when he opened his bag, there were ten thousand America dollars on the top. He smiled and thought, *"He was good to his word."*

Thomas loved Paris. He stayed at a flat near the hospital. He reported in, and they were glad to see him. No one noticed the time he had been in Jerusalem.

Everyday was a learning period for him. His day was busy, and he studied at night. He met a doctor about his age who was also learning and lived in Paris. His name was Emil Flocene. Emil invited him to his home for an evening meal. There he met his family. He had only one sister and no brothers. He sister's name was Mimi. She had huge brown eyes that made her beautiful She had a gorgeous smile and looked often at Thomas. After the meal, Emil said, "I want to take you to a show at the Moulin Rouge."

Immediately Mimi said, "May I go too, Emil?"

"Of course. Who would snuggle next to Thomas, I'm certainly not going to," and they all laughed

Mimi did just that. All during the show, she clutched his arm and put her cheek next to his shoulder. It felt good to Thomas. Thomas said, "You better stop that or I may have to take you home with me." Mimi smiled and clutched him tighter.

"How old are you, Mimi?" He thought she was about sixteen, but she said, "I'm twenty, and am already a widow. I was married when I was eighteen, but he had a terrible accident at work and I lost him. My mourning period is over now, and I'm looking for a lover."

Thomas was shocked and Emil could tell by the look on his face, so he said, "That's a Parisian woman for you. You had better watch out or she'll be in your bed before you know what happened," and they all laughed, but Thomas' laugh was a little sickly.

The three spent a lot of evenings together. Thomas never made a move on Mimi. And when Emil was using the facilities, she boldly asked him why.

Thomas said, "I have a sweetheart back in Dallas and cannot betray her."

"She would never know," said Mimi.

"Yes, but I would."

A serious look came on Mimi's face and she said, "I think I love you, Thomas."

"I'm fond of you Mimi, but not in love with you."

"Will you kiss me to make sure, Thomas?"

"Maybe sometime, but not here."

Two nights later there was a knock on his door. He answered it, and there stood Mimi. She said, "I came over to get that kiss, you promised me."

He invited her in and said, "I have some wine, would you like a glass?"

"Sure," she said, and plopped down on a chair. He brought out an Éclair that was delicious. She then said, "You know you could have two sweethearts. One for America and one for Paris. If I had you one night, you would understand the true meeting of love."

"I already understand the true meaning of love. I was

married once and I don't think any woman could make me love her more than her."

"Why aren't you with her?"

"Because Jesus took her to be with him. She is married to Jesus now as we all will be someday."

"I've thought about that. I bet being married to Jesus will be the ultimate love."

"I'm sure you're right. Then you are a Christian."

"Of course. I learned all the Bible stories as a child, and later gave my heart to Jesus. Mother still reads the Bible to us, all the time. She made both Emil and I memorize many verses."

"Then why would you sleep with me if we aren't married?"

"Because one night with me and you would want to marry me."

"Well, I'm not going to bed you, Mimi. I am going home soon, and you will be left here. Have Emil bring another doctor home. You'll find someone you will love who will love you."

Before she left, Thomas did kiss her. He was amazed as she kissed nearly like Lesley had kissed him. He liked it so much he kissed her again thinking of Lesley."

Mimi said, "See, you wanted more. If you slept with me, you would be in love with me."

She left and Thomas wondered if he could love her.

On the ship home he tried to compare Mimi to Mary, but they were too diverse in their personalities, and he couldn't compare them.

CHAPTER 14

AMERICA THE BEAUTIFUL

In New York City, he visited the Dowd family and even spent a night with them. He had to do some banking business, so he went to work with Dowd the next day. He met several of the old employees of his fathers.

He also went by the medical school and all had heard about his pioneering the plastic surgery world. He even gave a lecture on the subject trying to encourage some of the younger men to cast their lot that way.

There was now a railroad that ran from St. Louis to Springfield. Thomas knew a village that was just north of Ada and got off there so he could visit Ada. He rented a buggy and traveled to Ada. He stopped at Herb's store first and Herb nearly wrung his hand off, he was so glad to see him.

Herb said, "Come up to the house and have coffee, I want

to show you something. When Herb opened his front door a nice looking woman said, "Why are you home so early, Herb?"

Herb put on a big smile and said, "Thomas meet my wife. Give him a hug, Lara, Thomas is part of our family."

Lara said, "I am so sorry about your wife, Thomas. Herb told me how you loved her. We put flowers on her grave several times a year. Herb surely loved her. I came to Ada soon after you left. My sister is married to Joe Brooks, the banker. I came just for a visit, but when Herb and I saw one another, we both knew immediately. I would have bet anyone I would never marry again, but Herb swept me off my feet. We have been so happy together."

"It will take me only a minute or two to put the coffee on. I know you two will want to catch up on one another."

She left and Herb said, "What have you and Howard been up to these many years."

"It will be hard for you to understand, but I went through medical school before I went into the army. I took up that profession again in Dallas, Texas. Howard went through medical school there and is now a doctor, also. He is married and has a two year old boy.

I never remarried. I know Lesley would want me to, but I just can't do it, it seems."

Herb had tears in his eyes and said, "I miss that Lesley nearly as much as you do. She was a daughter to me as much as she was to Jim. I miss him, too. He had the best sense of humor I ever knew, but of course you knew that as you two joked a lot.

"I still can't get over the fact that you and Howard are doctors. I can't wait to brag about that around town.

"Did you know Braxton got married. He married Audrey Clemens' wife, Carrie. Audrey up and died about three months after you left. Another funny thing was that Braxton couldn't get anyone to build and run the general store, so he built it and runs it with Carrie. They're good store keepers, too. He don't need the money at all, but he loves to visit with people when they come in. Since Junior died, he's a changed man.

"Rowdy runs the ranch, and believe it or not he married that saloon girl, Sara, that Junior was so crazy about. One of the girls wrote her that Junior had hung himself, so she came back to Ada. Seems that boy, Doolin, was already married when she arrived in Texas.

"It took sometime for Sara to be accepted, but now she goes to church every Sunday with Rowdy, and everyone seems to have forgotten she was once a saloon girl. Heck, even Andrew Jackson married a saloon girl, so I guess it's okay."

Lara said from the kitchen, "I always wondered what it would be like to be a saloon girl. A different husband every night."

"That's my Lara, she says the darndest things anyone could think of. Keeps me on my toes, I guess.

"How long are you going to be in town, Thomas?"

"Just tonight. I want to get around and visit with the people I used to know. Is Cal Seagers still running the drugstore?"

"He surely is. We thought he would never get married again as he was so devoted to Emily. However, a woman came through town and became ill. She came to his drug store hoping she could get some medicine to help. She collapsed in Cal's store and he took her to his place and using some drugs, brought her to health. During that time they fell in love and married a short time later. No one thought he would ever marry again as he was so devoted to his Emily."

"I'll drop by and see him. You know he's responsible for me coming to Ada. I met him on a train going to St. Louis, and we bought a buggy there and came here."

"Yes, he told me that story several times, he, like several others, still talk about you. You made quite an impression on the folks at Ada."

Thomas left and went to the general store. He was met by a nice looking woman. She said, "I'm Carrie Braxton. Are you new in town?"

"No ma'am. I'm Thomas Benson and I used to live here some years ago. I just dropped by to see Bob. Is he around?"

"Oh, Oh! He told me about you. He said, you changed his life. He said, you were the best man he ever met. Oh, dear. He would want to see you. Are you going to be around for awhile?"

"No ma'am. I'm leaving early tomorrow. Tell him I still pray for him and now I'll include your name."

Thomas left and went to the drugstore. As he walked in Cal called to his wife who was in the back and said, Karen, come out here, the prodigal son has come home."

He shook Thomas hand and as Karen came out, he said, "Give him a hug, Karen, this is Thomas Benson. You remember me telling you about the man who came back with me one time."

"Yes, he's told me that story ten times at least, and I enjoy hearing it every time. He says you changed Ada from one end to the other. He said, That Bob Braxton used to be a terrible man, but you changed him. He's a wonderful man now. He helps everyone. He shocked people last year when he helped a colored family get on their way. They showed up broke, and there wagon had a broken wheel. He had their wagon repaired and filled them up with groceries. Everyone was astounded, as folks said he used to be very bigoted toward Negros.

"I just can't see him as a bad man, but the old timers assure me he was."

"Thomas returned to Cal's drug store and asked Cal, "Is Ruffins still the sheriff?"

"Lord, no. He gave that up about a year after you left. We have old man Kessler now. He couldn't break up a fight between two kids. The town keeps him on because he has to have the job to live."

After saying his goodbyes Thomas went over to the saloon. Larken was still there and remembered him and said, "Where's your partner, the gunfighter."

"He's now a doctor. He went through medical school in Dallas, and is married and has a boy."

My gosh. I figured he was a good guy. I lied to Sheriff Ruffins when he asked me if your friend were here all evening, the night Junior was hung. I'd heard about it, and thought if he done it, the town owed him a favor. You recon he hung Junior?"

"No Junior hung himself. The sheriff told me that Junior had no ropes to tie him and no gag. Everyone would have heard him if someone were to hang him. No, Junior hung himself."

"Well, the town surely don't miss him. I still remember the night that little cowboy beat the crap out of him. Everyone enjoyed that fight. The girls talked about it for months. They really enjoyed it. You know that girl Sara came back after Junior was hung and married, Rowdy James."

"Yeah, I heard. Anyone can change. I bet she made Rowdy a good wife."

"Let me buy you a beer, Benson. Everyone misses you around here. You're really the towns favorite son."

He drew him a beer and said, "Did they tell you that Bob Braxton rebuilt the general store and runs it now?"

"Yes, Cal Seagers told me. A person can change."

"Your telling me. I could hardly believe the change in Braxton. I've never seen a change in a man like that one. He's as humble as they get. He's really good at running that store. Everyone knows he doesn't need the money, he just likes doing it."

Thomas left and went back to Herb's place and said his goodbyes. He drove his buggy back to the village where he had rented it.

He caught the next train out to Tulsa. At Tulsa he found there was a train that ran to Dallas. He arrived home about the middle of the day and went directly to the mansion. All of the doctors were at work. He bathed and changed and crossed the street to the hospital. He went directly to Dr. Phillips office

CHAPTER 15

MARY'S TROUBLE

Dr. Phillips embraced him and asked him to take a seat. He said, "I have some bad news Thomas. Mary is in jail. Her husband put her there. After their divorce, Fred, got married again. Seems a woman he was seeing was carrying his child, and he had to marry her. They were married less than two months and she was found dead. She was shot through the heart.

Fred told the police he suspected his wife, as she was angry over him marrying another woman. The police went to Mary's apartment and found the gun that matched the bullet that killed Fred's wife. She could not account for the time that Fred's wife was killed.

She had gone home, because she had a bad cold and didn't want to infect her patients. During the time she was home,

Fred's wife was shot. Fred had an alibi that stood up in court. Fred accused Mary of cursing his wife the night before and threatened her life at Fred's house. No one heard the threats, However Fred convinced the police and the prosecutor, and they bought his story.

Her lawyer wasn't much good and she was convicted. She is set to go to that new prison in Jefferson City next week. None of us could figure a way to get her out of it. Several of us testified about her character, but none of us could convince the jury that she did not do the things, Fred said she did. She was sentenced to life in prison."

Thomas was shocked. He could just imagine what prison life could do to her. He made an instant decision. He said, "I need some time off before I go back to work. I need to talk to Mary and then see about her."

Thomas left without seeing anyone, not even Howard. He went to the jail and saw Mary.

She said, "I'm innocent, but can't prove it. I think Fred killed her and framed me for her death. He didn't love Beth, but married her because of the child. I didn't think he would go to that length to get out of being married to her, but I know he resented me for leaving him. I only met Beth once, and that was the night before the murder. I went over to his house to get a necklace that my aunt gave me. I had hid it because it was very expensive. I recovered the necklace and met Beth going out the door. We never said a word to each other.

The hack I used to go to his house, testified that he took me there and said he heard a woman shouting, but couldn't make out the words. That hung me. There's nothing you or anyone can do. Just pray for me. My life is over."

Thomas was resolved when he left Mary. He went to the mansion and just picked up his bag, as he had not unpacked. He told Hatti, the maid, he needed to take a trip. He said, "Tell Dr. Phillips I need to leave town for awhile."

He caught the train to Tulsa. He was lucky, because the train only traveled once a day and he just had to wait an hour when it left that day. He traveled to Tulsa then had to wait ten hours for a train going to St. Louis.

He traveled that train to a small village that was just twenty-five miles south of Jefferson City. He left the train there and found they had a stage that ran to Jefferson City. It did not leave until the next morning. There was a hotel that was very poor, but at least he had a bed for the night.

The next morning he was able to have breakfast, before the stage left. They traveled until dusk that evening and pulled into to Jefferson City. They had a decent hotel and he slept well that night.

The next day he traveled to the prison. It was a new facility. There were two sides to it. One for the men and one for the women. It was the only woman's prison in the state or many states. He was let out in front of the building. He was asked by a guard to state his business. He said he was there to see the warden on private business. He was put in a waiting room outside an office, and left there for about twenty minutes.

After that time, a guard came and searched him for a weapon and then said, "The warden will see you now." His guard had told the warden that a man in an expensive suit wanted to see him. The warden thought that maybe it was someone on the state prison board who was coming to see him. He was not frightened, but somewhat apprehensive.

When Thomas entered, the warden came from behind his desk and with a large smile said, "I'm Avery Johnson. How may I help you?"

Thomas said, "I'm Thomas Benson. I have come on a personal errand. Can anyone hear our conversation?"

Avery's antenna went up and he said, "I'll see. He pushed the door to the reception room where Thomas had been waiting, and nearly knocked the guard down who had his ear to the door.

Avery looked at him sternly and said, "Leave this office," and wait for me downstairs. I'll want to talk to you. The guard disappeared and Avery returned. Avery offered Thomas a seat and took one close to him.

Thomas said, "There's a woman slated to come here next week. She has been sentenced to life in prison. She is innocent, but was framed. I want to take her out of the country and I would like you to expunge all records of her coming here or ever being here. Is that possible?"

"Under the law, no. But I have complete control here, what did you have in mind?"

"I have ten-thousand dollars if you can make that happen."

"How do I know this isn't a frame up?"

"You don't, but I will show you the cash." Thomas brought out two stacks of hundred-dollar bills wrapped neatly. It was the money that the emir had given Thomas. The warden could tell that it was a considerable amount of money, ten thousand, perhaps.

"How would we do this.?"

Thomas said, "Her name is Mary Logan. You will probably have some correspondence soon about her being transferred from a jail in Dallas, Texas. They have no facilities for women in Texas and I found that she will be transferred here.

"When she arrives, you be downstairs to meet her at the gate. Take her to a room by yourself and give her a change of clothes that I will provide. I will come in a few minutes later and you will tell the guards that a man is coming to take custody of a woman prisoner. You can describe me and they will let me in. Have some paperwork that I will sign in front of your guards. I will then take the prisoner and we will leave. I will have a carriage waiting.

"Each one of these stacks of hundred dollar bills contain five-thousand dollars. If you agree I will give you one stack now, and the other when you hand me the papers I will sign. The money will be in a brown envelop that I will hand you. The flap will be open so you can see the money. So, do we have a deal?"

"Yes we do, Mr. Benson. I hope I never see you after the prisoner is gone. I want to know as little as possible. I can make it look like she is here, but never enter her name into the prison roster. Will she have visitors?"

"Not that I know of. If she does, tell them, she was transferred to New York soon after she arrived."

While Thomas was waiting in Jefferson City, he bought the clothes for Mary and rented a carriage that could be closed in. Mary arrived the next week and was asked by the warden to change clothes in a room near the gate. He took the manacles off her and handed her some clothes. He said, "Change into these."

The warden stood outside while she changed and then retuned and took her to the gate. A man who had a hat pulled low over his eyes handed the warden a brown envelope and signed some papers. The man then took her by the arm roughly and pushed her toward a carriage that was mostly closed in. He did help her in. They were driving away before she realized that the man was Thomas.

She sat in her seat and cried. They were a hundred yards away when she asked, "How did you get me out?"

"How else, I bought you. We have to hurry we have twenty-five miles to cover then board a train for St. Louis. From there we're going to New York, then on to Europe. I'm going to set you up there. You'll have to learn French, then you'll take their medical exam under an assumed name.

"I'll have to go back to cover my tracks. We'll be separated for a long time, but eventually we'll be together. I never told you, Mary, but I'm wealthy. My father was a banker and I inherited a lot of money. Not just a fortune, but beyond that. I'll set you up with a bank account and a nice place to live.

"I think we should live in Belgium. Is that alright with you?"

"Any place will be fine if we're together."

"That may be some time, but we will be together."

They traveled together to Brussels. He put her in a fine apartment, in the heart of town. He found an excellent tutor and she began her French lessons. He then left for America.

* * *

When he finally reached Dallas, he had been gone five weeks. Dr. Phillips said, "Where have you been? I bet it was to see Mary."

"Yes, she was transferred before she reached Jefferson City. She's now in a prison in New York and will probably be transferred again. They want her isolated."

"Well, I loved Mary, but life must go one."

Thomas met with Howard and they resumed their work. However, at night he worked on Mary's case. He had nothing to go on. He hired a lawyer, Harold Cramer, and he was able to obtain a copy of the court transcript. From that he got the name of the man who had testified he heard a woman shouting. He waited for the man to get off work and followed him to a tavern.

He sat next to the man at the tavern and learned his name was Niles Hampton. He was about forty. Thomas bought him a drink and introduced himself as Thomas Bisson. That talked about a number of things, but Niles did most of the talking.

He met Niles the next night and bought him several drinks. Thomas said, "I hardly ever read the newspaper, but there were several old papers left in my apartment. There was a story about a woman doctor who murdered the wife of her ex-husband. She must have been a cold one. The paper said she shot the wife of her ex in the heart.

"Did you follow that story?"

"Follow it hell, I testified at the trial. I drove the Logan woman to her ex-husband's house the night before the murder. The husband found out my name and gave me a hundred dollars just to say I heard a woman shouting, but could not hear what was being said. Easier money I have never earned. Anyway they found the murder weapon in her apartment, so I didn't have much to do with sending her up. We need people like that off the street."

"So you testified that you heard some woman shouting but didn't?"

"I tell for a hundred dollars I would say I heard president Johnson shouting."

Next Thomas had his lawyer ask what happened to the murder weapon. The police said they still had it and would not release it for ten years. He also found that the weapon was previously owned by Fred Logan. Fred had said that his ex-wife claimed to be looking for her necklace, but must have come upon his gun and stole it. He said he didn't know it was missing until after the murder when the police searched his house.

The transcript said that at that point, Mr. Logan said his ex-wife might have taken it while she was searching for her necklace. The police obtained a warrant to search Mary's apartment and found the gun.

The transcript gave out his wife's maiden name. Her name was Beth Abernathy. She was from Dallas. Thomas found where Beth's folks lived and paid them a visit.

Thomas said, "I am writing a book about the murder of your daughter, Beth. There could be some big money in it for you if you'll help me."

"How much money Beth's father said."

"Maybe five-hundred dollars if the book sells like I think it will. Will you help me?"

"Damn betcha! Will there be some upfront money?"

"No, but I will pay you twenty dollars for each interview. How does that sound?"

"Like money in the bank. When do we start?"

Thomas pulled out a twenty dollar note and handed it to the man and said, "Right now."

"Tell me how your daughter met Doctor Logan?"

"Beth met him at Sulley's, that bar on Fifth Street. She liked to hang around there. I never approved of her going there, but she didn't listen to me. She was hot-blooded and needed a man. Doctor Logan went with her just three times before she became pregnant. He was nice enough to marry her after I threatened a paternity suit. He agreed to marry her so I thought everything was alright.

"I had no idea that his ex-wife would become so jealous she would shoot Beth.

Fred didn't treat Beth all that good, and I could see he wouldn't stay with her after the baby was born."

"How could you know that, Mr. Abernathy?"

"I was over there one time and she said something he didn't like. He slapped her. Not just a little slap, but damn hard. He's a lot bigger than me, so I just had to let it pass. However, he showed his temper and that he didn't respect Beth."

"Could he have killed your daughter, instead of Mrs. Logan?"

Abernathy put his hand to his chin and said, "Yes, I think he could have. He would have the care of that baby until it was eighteen, and I could tell you, he didn't want to do that."

"Did he do anything else to Beth when you were in his presents?"

"No, I never went over there after that. They were only married a couple of months. However, Beth came over here and she told us how he called her names."

"She said, he called her a bitch and whore. She said if she had the money she would leave him. However, she cooked for him and cleaned his house."

"Thank you Mr. Abernathy. I don't know if we could put that in a book, but we could say he called her names."

Next Thomas traced the gun and where it was bought. The police hadn't done that. He found out that Fred had bought the gun ten days before the murder. He traced it through the serial number.

The gunsmith, Lance Pierce, who sold it to Fred said, "Yes, I remember the purchase, as it came out in the paper. It never said anything about how he came by the gun, but I knew and have a receipt. I keep a log on who buys guns from me and I have his name."

Thomas told everything he came upon to his lawyer, and Cramer logged all of what Thomas learned. He said, "Mr. Benson, we have more than enough for an appeal.

"Could we have an appeal without Mrs. Logan being here?"

"I'll talk to a judge and find out. It's unusual, but there's nothing she could add and she doesn't have to testify, so I can't see why not."

Cramer talked to a judge about an appeal. He said, "The woman in question is in prison. I see no reason why she should be at the appeals trial, if granted, as I will not call upon her to testify. It would just cost the state a lot of money. She will sign a statement that she doesn't want to be at the trial if you want."

"I won't require her to be there if you sign a statement waiving her right to be there."

The appeal was granted. Fred was furious. He cussed the prosecutor, and was livid. This did not endear him to the prosecutor.

At the appeals court, the hack was brought into the courtroom to testify. He could see Thomas sitting at the table for the defense and knew he was in trouble. When the prosecutor asked him about the shout, he said, "Now that I think about it, I don't really think the shout came from that house. It may have even been a man's voice."

The prosecutor was incredulous. He said, "But you said at the first trial it was a woman's voice you heard coming from the house that you had delivered Mrs. Logan."

"I might have said that, "But after I carefully thought it over, I changed my mind."

The prosecutor was exasperated and said, "You're witness."

Cramer said, "I have but one question. "You are now sure the voice came from another house. Am I correct?"

"Yes."

"Let it be known to the jury that no shout came from the house where Mrs. Logan was."

The next witness the prosecutor called was Fred Logan. He said, "Mr. Logan, the last witness stated the shouts did not come from your house. Didn't you say that Mrs. Logan shouted at your wife and threatened her life?"

"Yes, she did. I was standing right there, so I ought to know. I was appalled at the language that she ranted at my precious and dear wife"

"Thank you, Mr. Logan. Your witness Mr. Cramer."

"Would you say it was a hot day and all the windows here in Dallas were open as well as the doors?"

"It was warm."

"And the door is not over twenty-five feet from the place that Mr. Hampton was sitting?"

"Yes."

"Yet, Mr. Hampton heard no shouts."

"Well, maybe they weren't that loud. Maybe it was just the way she said it that made me think she was shouting."

"But no one heard those threats, but you, Mr. Logan. Didn't you make that up to take the heat off yourself."

Fred shouted, "I did not. My poor dead wife heard those threats."

"Only according to you, Mr. Logan, Only according to you."

The judge then said, "Is that all your witnesses, Mr. Carlson?"

"Yes, but I reserve the right to call others if necessary."

"It's your turn, Mr. Cramer.

Cramer said, "I would like to call the gunsmith who sold, as the prosecution termed, the murder weapon."

Please call Lance Pierce. Pierce was sworn in and Cramer said, You're a gunsmith are you not?"

"Yes."

Cramer handed the gun to Pierce and said, "Do you recognize that gun?"

Pierce read the serial number aloud and said, "Yes, I sold this gun to Doctor Fred Logan."

"Would you give us the date you sold it. Pierce raised a ledger and turned to the page he had logged the sale in and read out the date."

"Cramer said, "That was just ten days before the murder."

"That's all I have for this witness."

"Your witness, Mr. Prosecutor."

"No questions, your honor."

"The defense calls Clarence Abernathy." He was sworn in. Cramer then said, "Can you state what your daughter told you about her relationship with her husband, Dr. Logan?"

The prosecutor said, "Objection. Anything he says is hearsay evidence."

Cramer said, "I have his wife here who will verify what their daughter told them."

"Over ruled."

Abernathy then went on telling how their daughter told them he called her names like bitch and whore.

Cramer then said, "Can you tell the jury what happened when you and your wife visited the home of Fred and Beth Logan?"

"Beth said something he didn't like and he slapped her. Not a little slap, but a hard slap. I am much older and smaller than Dr. Logan, and could do nothing about it, so we left."

Cramer said, "And this is the man who called his wife precious and dear to the court. Mr. Abernathy has just shown you another side to Dr. Logan."

The judge said, "Save your remarks for your summation, Mr. Cramer."

The summation was short on the prosecutor's part. He said, "Mrs. Logan had ample time and opportunity to murder Beth Logan. She was in Dr. Logan's house the night before the murder. Although several hostile witnesses said things that may or may not be true. There is no doubt that Mary Logan murdered Beth Logan out of jealousy and hate."

When Cramer began he said, "What jealousy and what hate. Mary Logan had never met the woman. She had been divorced for over a year and was living a happy and productive life. Fred Logan had only known his wife for a month before she became pregnant.

"You have heard Beth's father testify that he and Beth's mother witnessed Mr. Logan slapping Beth Logan and calling her names. Where is the 'precious and dear' that Fred Logan called his late wife. Who had the motive to kill Beth Logan. Surely not Mary Logan.

I ask you why did Fred Logan purchase the murder weapon just ten days before the murder. I submit that Mary Logan had no knowledge of the murder weapon before the murder. The only person who had that knowledge was Fred Logan, who had ample opportunity to plant the weapon in Mary Logan's house. He's the one who told the police he was missing the weapon, and they should search Mary Logan's house.

"The first trial railroaded Mary Logan to prison. None of the evidence that was submitted today was even brought up at the first trial. I ask you to show justice and acquit Mary Logan."

The jury was out just a half-hour and acquitted Mary. The prosecution reopened the case again with Fred Logan as the accused. He was tried and found guilty of manslaughter as he copped a plea to prevent being accused of first degree murder. He was given ten to twenty years in prison.

CHAPTER 16

TRAGEDY

Thomas wrote Avery Johnson and included the transcript of the trial showing that Mary Logan was found innocent. He told Avery that keeping Mary out of prison was worth every dime he paid him.

Thomas traveled to Brussels to fetch Mary. It had been six months. She was ecstatic over seeing him. He told her about the trial and the speedy second trial, where Fred copped a plea for manslaughter instead of first degree murder.

Thomas said "He received ten to twenty year. Now lets go home."

They were only able to catch a sailing ship to England. It had two cabins for passengers. Just eight hours out of Antwerp a storm blew in. It started slowly, but increased rapidly. Mary immediately became queasy.

Thomas said, "I'll try to get some broth from the cook. It may ease your stomach. Their cabin was on the main deck. He opened the hatch and felt a tremendous gale. He had difficulty closing the hatch and preceded towards the galley. The wind was so fierce he had to hold on to a lifeboat to keep his feet.

Unknown to him, an ironclad steamship was bearing down on them on the other side of the ship. It struck them about mid ship. The ironclad vessel nearly went over them. The collision caused Thomas to be thrown into the bulkhead on that side of the ship with tremendous force. It left Thomas unconscious by the lifeboat. The ironclad vessel immediately backed away, and the wooden ship quickly began to sink.

Three sailors in the immediate vicinity had picked themselves up and were at the lifeboat in seconds. One saw Thomas and threw him into the lifeboat, then jumped in himself. The other two were busy unleashing the lifeboat and just as the water rose to the deck of their ship they moved the lifeboat away from the sinking ship.

From the time of the collision with the sailing ship and the backing away by the ironclad was only a minute or two. The sailing ship was underwater just as the ironclad came free of the sailing ship.

The ironclad ship looked for survivors and saw only the one lifeboat. It came along side the lifeboat and with great difficulty brought the four men aboard. Once aboard they were helped to a ward room where blankets were put over them and a hot cup of coffee put in their hands.

Thomas was now fully conscious as he sipped his coffee. He asked, "How many did you save from our ship."

"The mate helping them said, "Just the four of you. Everyone else went down with the ship. You four were just lucky."

Thomas thoughts then went to Mary. She was lost. Great sorrow came over him. The mate then said, "It was a quick death for them and that is a blessing."

Thomas was taken to a cabin that had two bunks. The other bunk was for the mate who had talked to them. When they were alone, Thomas asked where was the ship headed for. "We were headed for Iceland and then on to Newfoundland, but I understand that the skipper will go to England to make repairs."

Thomas always carried his money in a money belt when traveling, except for a few dollars that were in his wallet. He felt for his money belt and it was there.

He was given an officer's uniform to wear. After a hot bath and a shave he went with the mate to the galley.

He was greeted by the captain. Thomas told him his name, and said that he was an American. The captain said, "We could really use a doctor. Some of my chaps are in a bad way and we only have a medic.

Thomas said, "I'm a doctor."

The captain was almost gleeful as he looked to heaven and said, "Thank you, God!"

He led Thomas below to the hospital ward and Thomas began setting bones and sewing up wounds. The medic said, "That is the quickest my prayers have ever been answered. My name is Farley Grimes."

"I'm Doctor Benson, Mr. Grimes."

They reached London the next day. Thomas felt so alone.

He went to a nice hotel and sat in his room. He felt exactly like when he left the war. He didn't want to be with anyone. The tragedy was headlines in every paper. His name was listed with those lost as the one reporting thought everyone had perished. He had received that information from a spokesman who was not aware of the four men who had been rescued.

As Thomas read the paper he thought, *"I'll just stay lost. Howard can handle it, and train others. I need to be alone."*

In that same paper, he read an article about another tragedy at sea. *The SS Ville* du *Harve* had collided with the *Locke Evan,* and many people died. Aboard one of the ships was the wife of a financier, Horatio B. Spafford, from Chicago, and their four daughters. Spafford had stayed behind as he had some zoning difficulties of the property he owned and had to meet with city officials to clear up the matter.

The wife was saved, but the four daughters died. She sent a telegram that would later become famous. It said but two words: Saved alone. From this Spafford knew his four daughters had been lost. He was heartbroken.

"He left at once to join his wife. While aboard ship he wrote the famous hymen, *It is Well.* The entire hymen was printed in the paper, but it was the third verse that caught Thomas' eye. It said:

> *My sin, Oh, the bliss of this wondrous thought, My sin, not in part, but the whole, Is nailed to the cross and I bare it no more, praise the Lord! Praise the Lord! oh, my soul.*

Thomas was in tears when he finished reading that line. He thought, *"All the killing I have done, all the sins I have committed, was paid for by Jesus."*

He had lost his Mary, but Spafford and his wife had lost their four daughters. Still, the man thought only of Jesus and what he had done for him and mankind.

It put losing Mary in a different prospective and the burden of his loss was lifted somewhat.

* * *

As before he decided to go west and buy a few cattle and be alone for awhile. He thought, *"I wish Ed and Skillet were with me. I would like that."*

He stayed in London just long enough to book passage to New York. When he reached New York, he went to Union Station immediately and booked passage to Cheyenne, Wyoming. He had never seen the West and decided to see it.

The trip was just what he wanted. He was able to secure a Pullman. The meals were good and no one spoke to him but the conductor and the dining attendant. It took two days to reach Cheyenne.

It was a dirty town with mostly saloons. Thomas immediately bought a ticket on the next stage to Denver.

As Thomas was waiting for the stage to prepare for the trip, an old timer was waiting, also.

"He said, "Ain't you armed, Sonny?""

"I have a pistol in my valise."

"That sure won't get it done if were attacked by Injuns."

"Are we likely to be attacked?"

"Just as likely as not. The army's got the Sioux stirred up, and there are packs of them raiding here and there."

"Why didn't the stage company inform me of such a danger?"

"They don't tell anyone or few would take the trip. Most of us know the danger. Are you experienced with a rifle?"

"Some, I was in the war."

"I would get me a rifle if I were you. There's a gunsmith across the street there," and he pointed, "You best go buy one. It'll give us more firepower if we're attacked."

"Thomas thought, "I'll need one anyway if I buy a spread," so he walked across the street and went into the shop.

A man with a nice smile asked, "How can I help you, young man?"

"Do you have a lever action repeating rifle?"

"That I do. They're becoming very popular."

He turned around and brought out the rifle. He said, "It holds twenty-eight rounds. It cost twenty-five dollars, but I'll throw in two boxes of shells."

Thomas paid for them, put the boxes of shells in his coat pocket and walked back to where the old timer was.

The old timer said, "Now that's a good rifle. I hope you can use it. It will make us safer."

The stage pulled up and the passengers boarded. There were two ladies and two middle aged men, plus the old timer and Thomas. He stood back and let everyone board before he entered the coach. There was just one seat left and that was by the younger of the two women. She was about his age and her companion looked like her mother or aunt. The two other men both had side arms, but no rifle.

As they traveled, one of the men he didn't know said, "I hope we don't have any trouble. I left my rifle at home. I had it laid out, but forgot it, when I left. The other man said, "I don't think we'll have any trouble."

The older lady said, "What kind of trouble are you talking about, Sir?"

"Indian's, Ma'am. I was talking to an army officer last night, and he said the reason he was in Cheyenne was the army had dispatched him to lead a squad to search for bands of Sioux. Seems a passel of the young braves left the reservation, and are now causing trouble. He said the Army broke down their unites into groups of twenty as the Sioux raid in small bands of about eight to twelve warriors."

"Do you think we are in any danger, Sir?" The woman asked.

"Could be, but we have enough men to hold them off, I think."

No trouble came, but hours later as they approached the first way station, they could see they were under siege. The driver drove right toward the station as fast as the horses could go. He parked near the front of a building that was firing at the Indians.

The Indians pulled away when they saw the stage coach approaching.

It was nearing dusk. They entered the way station and a woman from within said, "I was wondering if they would send a stage. We're glad to see you, as we could have been overrun."

"The older lady asked, "Will they be back, tomorrow?"

"No way of telling that," said the old timer. Injuns are

a contrary breed. They take notions in doing things. They may figure we could hold them off or they might just try to overrun us."

The driver and the station's hostler went to tend to the horses. When they returned the hostler said to his boss, "They took the extra team, Mr. Poteet."

Poteet said, "That's bad. I think we need to keep a guard or two at the corrals tonight. They may come back and try to steal the other team tonight."

They were fed then Poteet asked the passengers to join in and help him guard the horses in shifts. No one wanted to do it, but Poteet said, "If you won't help me, you may be stuck here for a few days until the next stage arrives."

Reluctantly they were broken into four groups of two, to stand a two hour watch. Thomas was paired with the old-timer and they had the two to four a. m. watch.

The were wakened and were given a cup of coffee. They bundled up and went to relieve the men now on watch. When they arrived, Thomas said, "I think I'll go to the barn's roof. I can see the corrals clearly from there and beyond. I'll lie on my belly to keep from being outlined. You stay by the gate. Stay hunkered down so you can't be seen."

"You give orders like you were an army officer."

"I was a cavalry officer during the war." The old timer was impressed.

Thomas hadn't been on the roof over a half hour when she saw movement by some trees over two hundred feet away. There was a half moon, but it shed enough light to see, as it was a clear and cold night.

Thomas got his rifle ready. He saw two men come to the

side of the corral where the horses were. He waited until one of them ascended the corral fence then took the slack out of the trigger just as the Indian's head came into view.

The noise was loud. The other Indian made for his horse, but Thomas lead him and again pulled the trigger. The Indian fell and didn't move. Not a sound was made after that. Even the horses were quiet.

After fifteen minutes, the old timer said, "Did you get him?"

"Two," Thomas answered. Don't move until we are relieved. There may be others out there just waiting for us to move."

The people in the house were all up now. No lights were lit other than a candle that stayed lit. They only stayed up for about fifteen minutes. Poteet said, "Probably our men shot to make sure the Indians would not come." With that assurance, they all went back to bed.

At four the next watch came on. Thomas came down before they arrived to check the two Indians. The first Indian was shot through the head and the other through his torso. Both were dead. Thomas then checked where he had seen the movement by the trees. He could see where horses had stood by their droppings. He figured there were three and the one holding the horses took off when he saw his comrades go down.

The old timer looked at the Indians and said, "Sioux. Just boys it seems. It may make the others mad and they will come for us tomorrow. However, you cut down there size by two, so they may not come."

There were three braves in the group. The one with the

horses rode back to where their camp was and reported that the other two were cut down. He said, "I can't see how they did it. There must be more men that we thought."

"No, the leader said. They just were waiting for us. I know where Wikilunt and his ten warriors are. I'm going to ride there and try to get him to join us. They killed his son, so I think he will come." He left immediately.

By day break the warrior found Wikilunt. He told of his son being killed at the way station. He explained the number of men at the way station and the horses that they had. Wikilunt and his ten warriors went to the way station. It was three in the afternoon when they arrived. They decided on a strategy of firing arrows of fire to the roofs of the barn and station. Then waiting for the people to leave and pick them off.

However, when Thomas returned to the station he talked to Poteet. He said, "If they come again, they will now be very angry, as I killed two of their braves. They will try to burn the barn and the station. I'm going to be on the roof of the barn. I hope someone will go with me to cover all areas.

"If I were you, I would have a couple of men on the roof of the station to not only have a better field of fire, but to squelch fire arrows. You can probably have several buckets of water up there. I plan to do the same."

Poteet thought this was a good idea and he and his hostler went to the roof of the station. Thomas helped the old timer onto the roof and then passed him several buckets of water and two wet towels.

Fairly early the Indians shot arrows. Thomas could see them and methodically shot those in the open. However, they were now shooting the arrows from cover. The old timer used the wet towel and extinguished the arrows as fast as they hit the roof.

Poteet had another angle and also was able to kill an Indian. Wikilunk was furious. He hadn't counted on the men being on the roofs. He then gathered the warriors around him and said, "We must shoot those men on the roofs if we are to be successful. We will take the men on the barn first. If we can't shoot them at distance, we will rush the barn."

They tried to shoot the men on the barn from distance, but were unable as their rifles were poor.

They then rushed the barn. Thomas stood and as during the war, worked the lever of his rifle so fast it was hard to see his hands move. He killed six in twelve seconds, and the Indians drew back.

The old timer was in awe. He had shot, but didn't hit any of them as they were moving and he was not used to shooting at a moving target.

When they pulled back the old timer said, "My gosh! You're best I have ever seen. I can't believe my eyes. You shot half of their party."

"I don't think so, but we did cut their numbers down."

"Well, I only shot once and missed then."

"I think they will try to get someone in the barn to set it afire. Let me lower you down so you can surprise them."

He let the old timer down by one hand as he only weighed about a hundred and twenty pounds. Just as Thomas had suspected they had several moving from bush to bush and rock to rock. Thomas killed two of them, but one of them got to the barn. He had just lit a bush when the old timer shot him. He walked up and extinguished the bush. The other Indian was now back with Wikilunt.

Wikilunt said, "It is bad medicine here today. They have a fierce warrior among them. Let's wait until they are traveling again, then hit them while they are in a smaller group. We must make them pay for killing our brothers and sons. All agreed as they could see themselves being killed at the station.

CHAPTER 17

GETTING TO DENVER

They waited two more days and decided the Indians were not coming back. No stages came as the army had warned the stage company of the Indian trouble in the area. They packed up the third day and continued their journey. The horses were fresh and everyone was anxious to get going.

When they entered the coach, again Thomas waited until all were aboard before he entered. The seat that was left was between the old timer and one of the men. One of the men was sitting beside the young lady.

About an hour after they left, they were attacked by the Indians. The driver was killed and the shotgun rider now had to drive the coach. Bullets entered the coach and the man next to the young lady was shot dead through the wall of the coach.

Bullets entered the coach killing the older woman, and the man beside Thomas. The coach then turned onto it's side as the shotgun rider had been shot.

The coach skidded on its side until the horses broke free, then slid to a stop. Thomas knew the Indians would rush the coach, so he gathered his rifle and stood on a seat that had come loose. His head and shoulders were now above the side window, which gave him a view of the area. He could see them coming. He levered a bullet into the chamber and started firing. He killed two before they pulled off. He could see them running to a group of horses some two to three hundred yards away. He looked at the old timer and he was looking at the ceiling with a fixed stare. He was dead.

Thomas then looked at the young lady and said, "Our only chance is to go now and travel as fast as we can. You need to wear some pants or we can't travel as fast as we need to. Change into the old timer's pants, they ought to fit you. Put on all his clothes and wear his hat. She was just staring at him."

Thomas shouted, "Did you hear what I said!"

She then answered, "Yes, Sir," and began taking off her clothes.

Thomas pulled himself out of the coach. He went to the back and found a backpack. He rolled up three blankets and found a lantern with oil in it. He emptied his valise and strapped on his side arm. He put the lantern in it along with a hatchet, a large knife and another coat.

He went to the drivers seat and it was smashed. He could see a breadbox and knew there was food in it. He put that in the valise plus a bottle whiskey. He returned to coach and

151

looked in. The lady had just put on the old timer's pants and was putting on his wool shirt over her petty coat.

Thomas noticed she had good walking shoes. She now had the old timer's shirt on and was putting on his coat.

Thomas said, "Don't forget to put on his scabbard." She did that, then took his hat and put it on. He put his arm down and raised her to the top of the coach, then lowered her to the ground.. He got down and put the backpack on her, he took the valise and the blankets and they started walking.

They didn't walk on the trail back to the way station, but went west away from the trail that went south towards Denver. Thomas thought the Indians would expect them to return to the way station.

They walked until dusk. They came to a stream and followed it until they came to a bluff that would give them a wind break. There were several pine trees with an abundance pine needles. It was now too dark to travel.

Thomas took out the lantern and lit it. He could see that under the bluff was a cutout place like a cave. He put the lantern there, and then scooped up an arm load of pine needles, and put them in the small cave. The woman saw what he was doing, and began helping. They had never said a word since leaving the coach.

Thomas spread a blanket over the pine needles and the other two beside it. He then opened the breadbox and found several sandwiches. He handed the box to the woman, and she took a sandwich and sat down on a rock near the cave's entrance. Another rock stood beside that one, so Thomas took a seat beside her. They ate in silence.

When they were through with their sandwich Thomas said, "What is your name?"

"I'm Connie Sims."

Thomas said, "I'm Thomas Benson. We have a chance to make it. The Indians didn't know how many were on the coach, so they may not look for us. I'm not counting on that though. I have a couple of boxes of shells and can make it difficult on them if they find us. I was a cavalry officer during the war and can defend us."

Connie said, "Yes, I know. The old timer raved about how good you were."

Thomas said, "We must sleep together, but we have our clothes on so that won't matter, let's go to bed. We will have to get an early start.

Connie pulled off her shoes and hat and got onto the blanket Thomas spread the two blankets over her and crawled in beside her with his back to her. During the night he could feel her hug up to his back and it felt good.

Before first light, Thomas was up and packed everything. He looked at Connie and she had put on her shoes and hat and was rolling up the blankets.

She said, "This is most embarrassing, but I have never had to go to the bathroom in the wilds. What will I do.

Thomas said, "It's not that hard. Go behind a bush, then take down your pants and under pants. Bring them down past your knees and squat like this," and he bent down and showed her. "If you have to go big, use your hand to pull up some grass to clean yourself. We will be following the stream, and you can then wash your hands."

Connie said, "You are such a kind man. I bet you are a wonderful father."

Unfortunately, I have no children. My fist wife lasted only a few months as she was tragically killed. I'm a doctor and that takes all my time and energy, now."

"What kind of a doctor?"

"I am what is call a plastic surgeon. You have probably not heard of that. We try to build back faces that were destroyed during the war. I had a passion for this as I was in the war and racked havoc on the enemy so brutally that I will never be able to make up for what it did, but I try."

"My that is a noble cause. We must get you home at all costs. Even my life, if that is necessary."

"You have a tender heart, Connie. Are you a Christian?"

"Oh, yes. The woman beside me lead me to Christ. While we were walking I wondered why God spared me and took her. I finally came to the conclusion that God loved her so much, he wanted her with him."

"That is a wonderful thought. I was in battles where men on both sides of me were killed, but God spared me. I didn't know why until I saw the men's faces I was able to rebuild. I taught others and now they are doing my work."

"We need to go."

They traveled by the stream.

Connie followed Thomas and never spoke. They covered about ten miles and then Thomas said, "Let's get back to the trail. I feel the Indians have moved on. Actually the Indians had left an Indian behind to watch the coach. He had to relieve himself and had a bad case of diarrhea. He was gone while Thomas and Connie packed and left. They walked in a direction that put the coach between them and the Indian, so he never knew that anyone was there.

When Wlkilum returned the Indian reported no activity. They supposed the man shooting at them had died of his wounds as a rifle was beside one of the dead men.

That evening about dusk, they came to a way station. It was abandoned. Thomas decided it was safe to stay there. There was food in the house, and Connie fixed them a supper from the food left. That night, Thomas made them both good backpacks full of food. They were able to wash up and left with clean clothes the next morning. They had pillaged clothes from the way station's people. There must have been a boy staying there about the size of Connie and she was able to use his clothes. There were scissors and she asked Thomas to cut her hair very short, which he did. The old timer's hat now fit her well. She still wore the old timer's scabbard and Thomas asked, "Have you ever fired a pistol?"

She shook her head and Thomas said, "I'll give you some basic instructions. He showed her how to bring back the hammer with her thumb, then just pull the trigger. He said, "The only time I want you to use that pistol is if we are about to be captured. If I am unable to kill you, you must kill yourself. I don't mean to scare you, but you must never let the Indians catch you alive. They will torture you for days until they kill you. Do you think you can do that?"

"Yes, I understand. I will do it, but hope you will do it for me if that comes to be."

They slept in separate beds that night and were well rested for the next days hike. Thomas woke before dawn and they were off after a tasty breakfast. They again turned west and found the stream again and followed it. They stopped for lunch. Thomas had found a coffee pot and coffee, and packed it along.

After coffee and some beef jerky between slices of bread, they were off again. The stream was now on an intersecting angle with the trail. I was now running beside the trail.

About mid afternoon they came to a fair size village. There were soldiers there and other people who had come in to be safe. There was only one hotel. It was austere, but clean.

When they came to the desk the clerk said, "You're lucky. There is just one room left. Someone had to leave, just a few minutes ago. However, it's one of best rooms. You and your boy will sleep on a good mattress tonight. It's not a year old."

Thomas just said, "How much?"

"We get a dollar a night, now. How many nights are you staying?"

"That will depend on when the stage comes through."

"The stage has quit running due to the Indian uprising."

"Are their buggies for sale?"

"I'm sure there are. If you want to stay tomorrow night you will have to pay in advance as we don't hold rooms being they're in such high demand."

"I'll pay for two nights, just in case."

Thomas asked if there were hot water for bathing."

"No, we never had that. I think the barbershop may have hot water."

Thomas turned to Connie and said, "Let's put up our stuff and go get something to eat."

They did that and found a café not far from the hotel. The woman who waited on them said, "All I have is chicken and potatoes. With all the people in town they have cleaned us out."

The fried chicken and potatoes tasted good, as they were both hungry."

After eating they went to a livery stable. Thomas inquired about a buggy. The owner had several as many people had sold them to him for eating money.

They were able to purchase a buggy that had two seats. The dealer showed them how the back of the front seat folded down to the back to make a bed. It also had a cover that could be pulled up. It had sides that pulled down also and a rolled up cover for the front when they went to bed.

Thomas then looked at the horses. He bought a good one. The dealer said, "This horse was trained to pull this buggy. I bought them both yesterday from a doctor."

"How do you know he was a doctor?"

"He left his little black bag. I tried to find him, but he had bought a horse and left with a group of men."

"I'll buy the horse and buggy for the price you quoted, but I want the doctors, bag."

"Well, I have no use for it, so take it."

"Can you have the buggy and horse ready for tomorrow morning?"

"Yes, I can. What time?"

"About seven."

They walked back up the street on the other side this time. They came to a confectionary and Thomas walked in. He bought some chocolates at a high price."

Connie said, "Don't buy them, Thomas, there's too expensive."

Thomas said, "For my best girl, the sky's the limit," and he laid down a silver dollar.

As they walked away Connie said, "I might as well be your girl. I sleep with you every night. I just wonder what mother would say if she knew we slept together."

"She will never know unless you tell her. I don't see anything wrong with it. If you were a boy, like you look, it would be the same."

Connie said, "You've never asked me about my life. Why is that?"

"I figure if you wanted to tell me you would."

"Well, I will tell you all about me, if you will tell me all about you."

"It's a deal. We can tell each other everything, because when we reach Denver, we will probably never see each other again."

Connie said, I was raised in New Jersey. I had a normal home with two older brothers. My father was a musician and owned a music store. I just grew up like nearly everyone else, going to school and learning music from my father.

"I had a sweetheart and we got married about the time Fort Sumner was fired upon. He and my two brothers went off to war and never returned. My husband wasn't killed until the last year of the war. I didn't get word and just waited, but no word was forth coming. We got conformation about my two brothers, but my husband was just missing in action.

"I had moved back with my parents as they needed me when we got word about my brothers. They decided to move to Denver as they wanted to get away from everything. Dad bought a music store sight unseen and moved to Denver. I stayed with the house, as Dad said he might not like Denver and could always move back.

"I waited two years and then got conformation that Herbert had been killed. Daddy wrote for me to sell the house and come to Denver. It took a year to sell the house and here I am, sleeping with a man I hardly know. Now it's your turn."

"I want to know a little more about you. I need to ask some questions. Were you madly in love with your husband?"

Her face contorted some and she said, "I loved him I suppose, he was leaving for the war and he wanted to marry me before he left. I agreed, although I wondered if I really knew him that well. I think I know more about you than I did Herbert. I can tell more about you just watching and seeing how you treat me. You're tender with me and respect me.

"Most men would probably have come onto me as they slept with me. I knew immediately that you would never do that. Your compassion in helping other people pulled my heart strings. You have confidence and a manly bearing. I feel safe with you. Even when I thought we could be killed, I knew you would never let me fall into the hands of the Indians. I felt like your wife, much more than the week I spent with Herbert. You are twice the man he could ever be. Now tell me about your wife.

"I was only married a few months, but we loved one another. I still miss her laughter. I loved to hear it. We were building a house. A man who thought I had something to do with his son's death hired a man to kill me.

"Lesley and I were at the building site and she bent down to tie a shoe lace that had come loose. She raised up just as the assassin shot and caught the bullet intended for me in the head.

"I figured out who had hired the killer and thought about killing him. However, after thinking about it for awhile, I decided not to. It would not bring Lesley back. You see I killed sixty-seven men during the war that I know of. I tried to not keep count, but it was impossible. I decided I would not kill again at that point.

"I talked to the man before I left town, and told him I knew he had hired someone to kill me and accidentally had killed my wife. I told him I did not have anything to do with his son's death. I told him to live a good life, and to never fear retaliation from me. And you know what, he changed his life and now is the pillar of the community."

"I was in my senior year in medical school when they conscripted me. I, and the medical college, did our best to keep me out of the war before I finished medical school.

"It must have made someone angry for they put me in the infantry. I decided to be the best soldier I could be. I was good at my job. I ended up a major leading a battalion. I even met U. S. Grant at Vicksburg. He gave me an accommodation, not for battle, but for taking the initiative to have my men bury hundreds of men after that terrible battle.

"By accident I met my medical professors in Dallas and they encouraged me to help them start a medical school. I worked there a year until a woman doctor came to assist me. We worked side by side for a year, but I never looked at her as a woman. She was married.

"We were sent to Europe to observe and study plastic surgery, as it was new in America. In New York the night before we boarded a ship for Paris, she asked me to hug her. I thought it would just be a small hug, but she held me so tight and put her mouth to may neck and told me she loved me. I was instantly in love. I knew it was wrong. I told Mary that if we were to be lovers, our work would be over and hundreds of men who needed their faces reconstructed to have a life, would not get our help.

"She agreed and we were not lovers. After we returned, we helped many men who's faces needed rebuilding. We just scratched the surface in this work. I was asked to study for a year, learning the many procedures that were now being done.

"While I was gone, Mary divorced her husband. He took up with another woman and she became pregnant, so he married her. However he abused her terrible according to the woman's father. Two months after they married Mary went back to her husband's house to find a family heirloom that she had hidden. The next night the pregnant wife was shot and killed. Her husband claimed Mary had killed her and pointed them to search Mary's apartment where they found the murder weapon. She was tried and found guilty of first decree murder.

"I arrived back in America and found she was in jail, waiting to be transferred to a women's prison in Jefferson City, Missouri. I was able to keep her out of prison and took her to Belgium. I then returned and investigated the crime myself. I found several things that did not come up in her trial. In short I was able to get an appeal trial where she was exonerated of the murder. The prosecutor then reopened the case charging her husband with the murder. He saw they had the facts and pleaded to manslaughter and received a long prison sentence.

"I traveled to Belgium to return Mary home. We boarded the only ship available out of Antwerp and started home. We were only eight to ten hours out when a terrific storm hit us. A short time later an ironclad ship collided with us. I was going for some broth for her when the collision occurred. I was by a lifeboat and unconscious. Three sailors unleashed the lifeboat and I woke at sea. We were the only survivors. Mary was lost. It was reported that all were lost, so I decided to stay lost for awhile.

"I came to Cheyenne in hopes to go to Denver when you met me."

"Did you ever sleep with Mary?"

"No, we talked about it, but decided to wait and be married. Of course that never happened."

"So you only slept with two women."

"No, just one."

"You aren't counting me."

"That don't count."

"Well, the night is young," she said with a twinkle in her eye."

Their trip went well. They had no trouble and made it much faster than by stage.

Thomas took her to her father's home and she introduced him to her parents. He didn't stay long and was on his way.

CHAPTER 18

FINDING A SPREAD

Denver was much different. It was fairly clean and had a nice hotel. It even had a floorshow. It wasn't much good, but the food was good.

After the show, he went to the bar of the hotel. There was a nicely dressed gentleman about fifty standing having a brandy. Thomas said, "Do you mind if I joined you?"

"I would be honored," the gentleman said.

"I'm Thomas Benson and I came west to buy a small spread. I don't want to run over fifty head, just enough to get by."

The man smiled and said, "I'm Bob Murphy. I hale from Laramie, Wyoming.. I own a large spread and wish it were what you just described. Unfortunately I have a large family who depend on me. I employ twenty-two cowhands and run about three thousand head or more. We never counted them. They're spread over several miles.

"Yes, I wish I could trade places with you. You go run my place and let me find that small spread with very little worries."

Thomas smiled and said, "No thanks Mr. Murphy, I need to be alone for a year or so. The war nearly burned me out, and now I've lost my woman. Actually two women. I lost my first wife, also."

"I don't mean to sound unsympathetic, but losing my wife would not be that much of a tragedy. She's on me day and night about our children. I can't do anything with them, they're grown. I did my best, but was always too busy to see that they grew up right. Oh, they're alright, just spoiled, and don't have any direction.

"I surely didn't mean to lay my troubles on you, Mr. Benson."

"It's alright, Mr. Murphy. I think it does a body good to just layout his troubles, and get them off his chest."

"You sound like a man from the East. Do you know anything about running a ranch?"

"Some. I had about a section of land down near Springfield, Missouri for about two years. I had a colored man that helped me. He taught me the trade. He was one of the best friends I ever had, and I miss him and his wife. Her name was Skillet. Can you beat that?"

Murphy smiled and said, "I'm afraid I can't, but I wish I had known them. They sound like good people. What happened to your woman, if I may ask?"

"The first one rose up from tying her shoe and caught a

bullet in the head meant for me. The second, some years later, drowned when a ship collided into ours."

"Yes, I read about that, but it said, "All the people were lost.""

The reporter just got that wrong. Four of us survived. I was knocked down and was thrown into a lifeboat with three sailors. We were the only ones who made it. I was a doctor and my last woman was a doctor, also. It was a terrible loss. Not only was she a great friend and partner, but I loved her dearly."

"You know, Benson. I don't have any troubles at all. All my people are alive and healthy. I think when I get home, I'll pick my wife up and kiss her deeply. I'm gong to call all my kids to come over and hug each one of them.

"I do know some country that would suit you. You don't want to come to Wyoming. Every ranch up there runs thousands of head. However, there is a place in southern Colorado, in the western part of the state that had rolling hills and lots of grass and water. It's called the Tonto Basin by some. It's west of a place called Canon City. A small ranch could do well there."

"Thanks for the advice. If it gets too bad in Wyoming, drop down and see me. I bet you could help me a lot."

"I'll keep that in mind, Benson. Don't be surprised if you see me ride up someday." They shook hands and departed.

The next day Thomas went to the land office and talked to a clerk about the area known as the Tonto Basin.

The clerk said, "That area has many names. But the man told you right. It would be quite suitable for a small ranch. I've been through there. I've heard rumors of many outlaws and renegade Indians in that area, so you had better check that out before you put down hard cash."

Thomas thanked the clerk and bought some maps of the area. He took his buggy and horse and headed south the next day.

He went to Colorado Springs and looked around. He spent a couple of days there as the area looked pretty nice. He was at the hotel saloon and was standing next to man who was telling the man next to him that he was heading for Canon City the next day.

The fellow said, "I'm going to set up camp in Canon City, then go prospecting."

His friend said, "Look out for outlaws. There are plenty around that area. Just north of Canon City is Cripple Creek and they discovered silver there. I bet there's a thousand people around that country looking to be rich. That has attracted men who don't work for a living other than robbing people. You better be quick with a gun and keep your eyes peeled. I sure wouldn't go in that area without a partner."

His friend left and Thomas said, "Do you have a partner?"

"I did, but he got himself shot last week. He just couldn't keep his mouth shut. I told him a dozen times, but when he drank he couldn't shut up."

"I'm Thomas Benson and was planning to travel to Canon City tomorrow and I don't have a partner. Would you care to ride with me?"

"That's mighty neighborly of you. I'm Tom Watson. I'm a prospector. I've been mighty lucky in the past, and hope to live in Canon City, then travel from there to look around the country for a likely place. The way I hear it, there are still some renegade Indians around that area and the country is full of outlaws. I'll need a partner, at least until we make it to Canon City. Are you handy with a gun?"

"I was a cavalry office for four years during the war."

"Well, that makes me feel a tad safer. You'll do to ride with. I'll tell you what, I'll meet you at the livery stable about an hour after sunup."

"Is there a descent trail? I like to travel in a buggy. I can sleep off the ground and it has a cover I can pull up if it rains. I can also carry a lot of things and don't need a pack horse."

"Yeah, there's a descent trail as the stage goes to Canon City from here. That sounds like the way to travel. However, if you're a prospector, a buggy won't take you where I plan to go. What do you plan on doing in Canon City?"

"I'm going to scout round for a place to run about fifty head of cattle, and just live off the land."

"Man needs a woman to do that. Me, I had a couple of women, but neither stayed with me because I moved too often. One ran off with a salesman, and the other went back east to her mother. After that I just used the saloon girls. It's cheaper in the long run with no arguing, except over the price."

Thomas was up early and was at the livery stable about an hour after sun up. He had his handgun strapped on and his Winchester with several boxes of shells. He also bought provisions for a couple of days and a bedroll.

They were off by eight and the morning was delightful. The sun was shining and the air fresh as a mountain spring. They traveled until noon, then stopped and built a fire. The had coffee and some sourdough bread with some side meat.

Tom said, "I can't think of anything that side meat don't make taste better. I take a slab with me where ever I go."

"Yeah, you're right. I hear raising hogs is lucrative, however, the smell keeps me from raising them. I'll just buy from others."

"Well, I'm never in a place long enough to raise anything. I have to keep moving in my profession."

That night they found a camping place off the trail some by a fast water stream. They finished the common chores and were eating, when they heard horses riding up.

Tom said, "You greet them and I'll get behind that rock there."

In just a minute or so the horses rode up. It was three young men. They came to a halt and said, "How about sharing your supper with us?"

"No," said Thomas.

"Now that's not very neighborly of you. Maybe, we'll just take it from you."

The obnoxiousness of the boys began to bring up the ire in Thomas that had lay dormant for awhile. It began to grow in him and he again became the man he was during the war.

"If you move a muscle, I'll kill the lot of you."

"A tough guy are you. Maybe we'll just take what we want."

A rifle fired and knocked off the hat of the person doing the talking."

"It had a chilling affect."

Thomas said, "Ride on now. I know what each of you look like. If I see you anywhere, I'll shoot you dead on the spot without warning. We're heading for Canon City and if I see you there, you had better draw iron because I will be."

The three just rode off towards the west. As they were

riding one of the men said, "Bobby Lynn, let's go back to Colorado Springs."

"No, I want to dry gulch that smart mouthed hombre."

The third man said, "He'll kill you Bobby Lynn, that's no man to fool with. We don't even know how many there were."

"I don't care. No man takes my hat, without paying dearly for it."

"I'll buy you a new hat, Bobby Lynn. It's not worth being killed over."

"If you say another word, I may just kill you. We're going to get them tomorrow and that's that."

No one said a word after that. They rode on for another five miles then pulled up to a stream and spent the night there.

After the three were gone, Thomas said, "That's not the end of this. They'll be lying for us up the trail."

Tom said, "What should we do."

"Out wit them of course. Let's stay here another day. They will want to know what happened to us, and come back this direction. I'll hide the buggy and when they get abreast of us we'll get the drop on them."

"You mean shoot them in cold blood?"

"What do you think they would do to us if we travel on?"

"I'm not killing anyone in cold blood."

"Okay, I'll let them kill you first then I'll kill them."

Tom didn't like it, but he knew Thomas was right. They set up in an area where the three had to ride through. There were shear rocks that bordered the tail in that area. It was a short stretch of about fifty feet. The plan was for Thomas to step out and block the trail. Then Tom would come out behind them. If they went for their guns it would be a shootout."

Just like Thomas predicted, the three came the day after they rested for a day. They could here them talking as they rode.

Bobby Lynn said, "Just as I told you, they got scared and went back to Colorado Springs."

Thomas stepped out and said, "No, we didn't." Bobby Lynn went for his gun and Thomas drew with lightening speed and shot him through his middle, Bobby Lynn was dead instantly. The other two just sat there with pale faces shaking."

Thomas said, "We have a shovel. Go bury your friend. I was going to hang you, but I'll let you go if you swear you will never come this way again. If I ever see you again, I won't kill you. I'm going to shoot you in both knees, and you will be a cripple the rest of your life. Now get that trash in the ground." His icy tone was like death talking.

As the boys were digging, Tom said, "The war made you a vicious man, Thomas."

"Actually I'm trying to get over that. I just talked that way to make a point to those boys. They will remember what I said, and probably won't come this way again. Otherwise you might be prospecting someday, and they would ambush you. You can't be easy on people who are evil."

When they reached Canon City, Tom left Thomas without a word. Thomas thought, "That man has been lucky. I don't see him living a year in this country."

Thomas took his rig to the livery stable, and the hostler tended his rig and horse. He took his bag and crossed the street. He found a hotel that seemed to be okay. He asked for their best room.

The clerk smiled and said, "I have just the suite for you, Sir."

Thomas signed the register and a boy appeared and took his bag. Before he left Thomas asked, "Does the hotel have a dining room?"

"Yes we do, Mr. Benson. It's just down that hall," and he pointed. "They have a show at seven."

Thomas took a bath and shaved. He put on an expensive suite, combed his hair neatly and went down to the dining room. It was nearly full, but the headwaiter had been tipped off and knew Thomas, as he had been described.

He took Thomas to the edge of a stage in the center, and sat him at a small table with a linen table clothe. He said, "Would you care for some wine, Sir?"

"Yes. Do you have an Éclair?"

"We do, Sir. "It's from France, and is very expensive. It cost three dollars a bottle."

"That's okay if it's good."

The waiter brought him the wine, opened the bottle and poured him a sample. Thomas swirled it in his glass, then smelled it. It was delicious. He smiled and said, "That is excellent. I think I'll have a steak. I want it pink on the inside."

He had just finished his meal and was drinking another glass of Éclair when the band struck up a number, and the curtains were drawn. A beautiful woman appeared in a gown that complimented her. She sang a couple of Steven Foster's tunes. The first was *Beautiful Dreamer*.

About halfway through her song she gazed at Thomas and then never took her eyes away until the end.

The waiter was back and Thomas asked, "Who is the woman singer?"

The waiter had a shocked look and said, "Why that's Lillian Gayle. I thought everyone knew her."

"I've been abroad for sometime. Would you tell her that I would like her to join me?"

The waiter was further aghast. He said, "How would I do that?"

Thomas said, "That's easy. You just walk backstage and tell someone, you have a message for Miss Gayle. Then deliver it. Here's a dollar for your trouble."

The waiter left. About ten minutes later Lillian appeared at his table. She was about five-six and had a beautiful figure. Her auburn hair went to her shoulders, and she had big brown eyes. Not as big as Mimi's, but large, and she wore a gorgeous smile.

Thomas got up and took her hand and said, "I'm Doctor Benson. I was intrigued with your singing and wanted you to share a glass of Éclair with me. Would you do that?"

"I will, Doctor. You remind me of my ex-husband. He couldn't put up with my travel, and told me that it was either him or my career. I told him that was an easy choice."

"Are you engaged with someone now, Miss Gayle?"

"I guess I am, I'm having glass of Éclair with you."

The waiter sat her in a chair opposite Thomas and poured her wine.

Thomas took his seat and said, "I would like to get to know you. I'm new in town and didn't have one friend until now."

"I feel the same, Doctor Benson. I've been here two days and have not made a friend. I saw you during my first song and was enamored. My ex-husband was handsome like you, but I find it's what's on the inside of man that really makes him handsome or not. Are you married, Doctor?"

"Widowed, Miss Gayle. That's why I am in Canon City. I wanted to be away from anyone I knew and start over again."

"I won't ask for more details now, as I'm sure you valued her deeply."

"You are astute, Miss Gayle. She was my best friend and partner."

"I've not been as lucky. My career left me with only superficial suitors, until I met Ralph. He was the jealous type. If I had known that earlier, we would have never married, for you see, in show business you're naturally hugged and kissed often."

"I must get into show business that sounds like something I would like."

She laughed and said, "I like you, Doctor, can we use first names?"

"I would like that, call me Thomas and I will call you Lillian."

"No, that's my stage name, I would like you to call me Cindy, like my mother used to do."

"I would like do that, Cindy. It has a ring to it, like making someone happy."

"I hope to make you happy, Thomas. Does anyone call you, Tom?"

"No, my mother and father forbade anyone to do that. It didn't bother me, as I always wanted to please, mother."

"You must have been devoted to her."

"She was my best friend. You can't begin to know how much I loved her."

"Is she still alive?"

"No, a sickness took her soon after the war."

"But you met your wife who took your mother's place."

"No one could take my mother's place, but she was very close."

"Were you married, long?"

"Actually we were never formally married. We were intending to marry when she died."

"What was her name?

"It was Mary Logan."

Can you speak of it."

"Yes. She was drowned in a shipping accident in the North Sea some months ago."

"Oh yes, I read about that, but the paper said there were no survivors."

"I know it said that, but the report was wrong. I was knocked unconscious near a lifeboat. A sailor threw me in. Four of us survived."

"Then you've never been married."

"Actually I was married soon after the war. However, there again, it had a tragic ending. We were married for only a few months. We were building a house. Her shoe came untied, and after retying it, she raised up and took a bullet meant for me."

"How tragic. You have had some terrible luck. I hope I'm not in danger."

"No, we're not in love."

"Yet," She laughed.

Thomas said, "Then where do we go from here?"

"You call on me after every show, and we spend a lot of time together, build a white house with a white picket fence and have three kids."

"You're something, Cindy."

"What do you plan on doing here, Thomas?"

"I had intended to find a small ranch near Canon City, stock it with a few cows and live a solitary life. However, like most of my plans something happens, and my plan go awry."

"Are you staying in the hotel?"

"Yes, room 102."

"We're next door to one another, I'm in 101. I believe there are connecting doors inside. Could this be Karma?"

"I guess we'll find out. I thought I would grieve for at least two years before even looking at another woman, but then you came into my life with a bang."

"I feel the same way. I had no intention of seeing another man, but the moment I saw you, I had a feeling we would meet. Do you remember me looking at you when I sang."

"Yes, that's why I asked you to my table."

CHAPTER 19

CINDY WILLIAMS

Cindy had another show to do so, they parted. Thomas went back to his room. He had several medical journals that he wanted to read. They were in French, but he now read French nearly as well as he did English. He must have read for two or three hours and had just laid down the journal, when he heard a knock at his door.

He answered it, and their stood Cindy. She said, "Let's have a nightcap. He pointed to chair he had been sitting in, and before she sat she picked up the medical journal he had been reading and said, "My, you must be educated to read French magazines. Do you have some sherry?"

"No, but I can order some."

"Don't do that, I have some in my room. Come with me. She went to the connecting doors and found it was locked.

She turned and said, "I see you locked the door. Very prudent. I might try to take advantage of you," and Thomas smiled.

He was wearing a smoking jacket that was upscale. It was made of felt with golden trimmed lapels. It also had his initials over the breast pocket. He had it made in Dallas.

Her room was lush. They had decorated it lavishly, and there were several stands with flowers. She pointed to the coach for him to sit. It sat in front of an unlit fireplace.

There were logs accompanied by the paraphernalia used to make it easy to light a fire.

Thomas asked, "Would you like me to light a fire?"

"Yes, please. Do that while I change."

They both finished at about the same time. He turned to see her. She was wearing a robe, not much different from his smoking jacket. It was a dark gold velvet with sliver trim. It was open enough to show her ample breasts. He could see the legs of her pajamas underneath."

He said, "My you are a delight to see." She was busy getting the Sherry and glasses. She came to the table in front of the coach and poured each an ample amount in their glasses.

"She said, "That fire feels good. Here we are in a hotel room together in our night closes in front of a warm fire. Just think we have only known each other a couple of hours. I would bet it took you months to get to this point with Mary?"

Actually it was a couple of years or more. When I first met her, she was married to another doctor. We worked together in surgery many hours. As she was married, I never looked on her as a woman. She was just my partner and fellow doctor."

"I bet she didn't see it that way."

"No. We were assigned to take a trip to France to observe

some skin grafting techniques. We had to wait a few days in New York City to catch a ship. I had lived in New York City most of my life, so I knew everything that was going on. After we had dinner, I took her to a drama the first night. As we were going to our rooms, she asked me to give her a hug. I thought it would be a quick hug, but she clung to me tightly and put her face to my neck. When we pulled apart, I was in love.

"However, I explained that we could not love one another or it would destroy all the work we had done and cause a terrible scandal. She acquiesced and it stayed that way for another year. I don't know why I'm telling you all this, I barely know you."

"Because we both know that we will part soon, and have to live three years in two days. It's just the way it is. We have both found someone who we are extremely attracted, and must move fast or not have what we both want."

"And what do you want?"

"I want to be loved and cherished. My work keeps me moving. I'm due in Denver next week. I want you with me. I want your arms about me and to feel loved."

"I can't do that, Cindy. I have to establish myself someplace. I told you my plans."

Will you at least meet me in Colorado Springs in two weeks. We're doing a show there over the weekend." Her eyes were pleading, so he nodded and then kissed her."

They sipped their sherry and then Thomas said, "I think I will go back to Colorado Springs and look around there for a place. It's further from the mines and all the riff-raff that comes with them. It appeared to be much more civilized, than Canon City."

Thomas returned to his room about a half-hour later. He could tell she wanted him to stay, but he knew the deadliness of that, and left.

They had breakfast together the next morning. She was leaving, and he decided to leave also.

They had returned to their rooms and Cindy came through the connecting doors and said, "Kiss me goodbye and promise me you will see me in Colorado Springs in two weeks."

Thomas nodded and kissed her.

* * *

He waited until the next day to leave. He had decided to follow a stagecoach for safety. He told the stage driver he would be behind him. The stage driver said, "That will be safer for us both. The trip was easy. They stayed midway at a way station.

Thomas became acquainted with the passengers. All new he was following the stage. An older woman, probably in her late forties asked, "Would you mind me riding with you the rest of the way, Mr. Benson. It is so cramped in the coach. It will give all of us more comfort."

Now Thomas didn't want to do that, as he liked his solitude. It gave him time to think. However, he could find no words to get out of it, so he said, "I would be pleased, Mrs. Emory."

As they traveled the next day, Mrs. Gladys Emory asked, "Are you going to stay in Colorado Springs, Mr. Benson?"

"I really don't know. I have an acquaintance that I am meeting in a week or so, then I will decide. If I do stay, I would like to buy a small ranch close to town. It will require a house. I will just have to see how Colorado Springs suites me. I was going to locate in Canon City, but it's too close to the mines and you know the element that comes with miners."

"Indeed I do. My sister, who I visited, filled me in on the wildness of that place. I was appalled.

"We have parties now and again in Colorado Springs. My husband is a councilman, so he has to attend many of those functions. I would like you to attend so I could introduce you to some of my friends. You being a handsome young man will make their tongues wag, when I tell them that I rode with you from Canon City. I'll send you an invitation in care of general delivery at the post office."

Other than brief conversations that noted the landscape and weather, not much conversation was made. Thomas enjoyed his solitude. Before they arrived at Colorado Springs, Thomas asked about a land agent.

Mrs. Emory, told him of a man named Charles Lane, who was a friend of her husbands, and was engaged in that work.

They parted at the stage station and Thomas went on to the only hotel in town. It was large and fairly nice. He told the clerk that he wanted the best suite, available, as he imaged that Cindy would stay near his room.

After checking in, he went to Charles Lane's land office. He explained what he was looking for.

Lane said, "You came at an opportune time. I have several places that people want to sell."

"Lets start with the closest place to town, and then move out from there."

There was a place not two miles out that had four hundred

acres that was close town. The house was immense, but was in disrepair as was the barn. It did have a good windmill and raised tank to take water to the house and barn.

"The man tried to farm it," Lane said, "But the rocks and rolling hills were not conducive to farming. However, there are about twenty acres that can be farmed. He fenced that area to keep the critters from ruining his crops.

"Being it is in such sorry shape, no one wanted it. It's been on the market for over a year. I think you could get it for about a thousand dollars, which I believe is about right."

"Let's look at the house." The house had a porch that ran completely around the front and two sides. It was two storied. They entered into a large room whose ceiling went to the roof. There was a stair case that went to the second floor. The rooms that faced the great room had an open hallway with a railing that surrounded the great room except for the front. Everything needed painting as it had sat idle so long. Although it needed painting the integrity of the wood look good. It had six bedrooms, upstairs, and three down stairs, but no bath. It's kitchen was large, but antiquated as they cooked in the living room from the hearth. Thomas thought he could renovate the house and modernize it if he could find a good contractor. He could use one of the bedrooms between the rooms to make back to back bathrooms to modernize the ground floor, and do the same with the bedrooms upstairs so everyone would have their own bathroom. The kitchen would have a new stove and new counters and cupboards.

They went to the barn and it was in bad shape, also. However the wood was in good shape. He could re-roof it and put in stalls, watering troughs and feeders.

After the renovations to the structures, he could have it fenced. The pastures were good and it had a year-round stream through it.

Thomas said, "I'll tell you what I'll do. I'll give you fifty dollars as earnest money to hold it for me at the price you named for one month. It will take me that long to go over my finances. At the end of a month, I will tell you whether I will take it or not."

Actually, Thomas had over seven thousand dollars on him in his breast pocket.

Lane said, "Let's go back to my office and sign some papers to keep this legal."

As they were driving Thomas asked, "Do you know any contractors who build modern houses?"

"Yes. We have a expert builder, named Bob Britton. He's from back East and came out here for his health. Actually he's an architect and his brother does the building. He knows all the modern methods and appliances. If you want to see his work, go look at the new playhouse that is across from the hotel."

Thomas had seen the new structure, but hadn't paid close attention. After they had signed the papers, Thomas went to look at the new playhouse. It was closed, but he went around to the side and a door was ajar there.

He walked through the door and met a maintenance attendant. He said, "I would like to tour the playhouse and look at the workmanship. I'm thinking of renovating a house and I want look at Mr. Britton's work."

The attendant said, "You will be awed." He took him first to the bathroom. It had tile on the walls and floor in brilliant colors. The sinks were marvelous and the toilets were enclosed and made of porcelain. The walls of the building had wainscoting to four feet then cloth on the walls with felt designs of women who where scantly clad. It had carbon lamps that could shine on the stage as bright as sunlight. There were many features that Thomas had never seen before. He was shown a heating system of steam.

In the basement was the furnace that fueled the steam heaters. The coal oil lamps could be turned up and down with a central lever. Thomas was impressed.

He thanked the man and left for Bob Britton's office. He found him there. He entered and said, "Mr. Britton, I am seeking a builder to renovate a large old house and barn that I may purchase. If I buy the place, I will want to renovate the house and barn with all the latest conveniences. I will give you fifty dollars earnest money to show me what you can do and give me an estimate, if you take the job."

"Oh, I'll take the job. Things have been slow around here for about a year. I did get some work with the new playhouse and the new Johnson home to keep me afloat. Let's go look at your place. We'll use my buggy."

When Britton looked at the house and barn he smiled and said, "I love this type of work."

When they were in the house, Thomas said, "I want to use the bedroom between each bedroom to put side by side bathrooms, so every bedroom has its own bathroom. I want a modern kitchen with all the latest appliances and a new heating system that will keep us warm through the coldest of winters. All the windows will have to be replaced and new doors to the outside unless you can renovate the old ones. Then a complete make over inside and out."

"You're talking some serious money, Mr. Benson."

"Can you give me a rough estimate with in a thousand dollars?"

Britton thought a minute, but he had a quick mind. He said, I would roughly say five thousand dollars give or take five hundred. Is that within your budget?"

"Yes, I thought it would be more."

"I'll work up a cost estimate and try to have a few sketches so you will have an idea what it would look like. I can do that in a week's time."

"Marvelous. Now let's go look at the barn. That's going to cost another thousand, I'm sure."

"I surely hope you take this place, as I love this type of work."

Thomas said, "Spare no cost. I want this to be a show place. If possible I would like fire places in the bedrooms. The largest bedroom will be mine and I want you to make it where a queen would feel at home."

"Keep going Mr. Benson, I'm nearly foaming at the mouth. If we do the job, I will want to show it to future customers. I'll lower my price considerably if you will agree to that."

"Yes, I would like that too, it will give me some status in the community."

Saturday came and just like Thomas thought, Cindy was put next to his suite. It did not have connecting doors, but was next to him. He was in the lobby reading a journal when she came in. She had an entourage with her of about ten people.

When she saw Thomas she ran into his arms and kissed him. The people with her were stunned as she had never mentioned anything about Thomas. She turned and said,

"This is my dear friend, Doctor Thomas Benson," then said, "I won't name each one of my friends as you would never remember their names. However, I hope you will know all of them by the time we leave for Pueblo."

Thomas nodded to them, then helped Cindy with her luggage. When they were entering her room, Thomas said, "I have the suite next to you, but there is no connecting door. She put on a coy look and said, "That's okay we may just require one room."

Cindy had rehearsal that afternoon and a performance that night, one at seven and one at nine. They performances lasted, just over an hour.

It was Friday and Thomas went by the post office and checked his mail. There was an invitation from Mrs. Gladys Emory inviting him that night to a party at her house. It gave the address, so Thomas drove his buggy over to her house and knocked on the door. A servant opened the door and Thomas said, "Dr. Benson to see Mrs. Emory."

Gladys said, "Oh, I am so glad to see you, Dr. Benson. Did you get my invitation?"

"I did, Mrs. Emory. However, I cannot be here until after ten. An associate, who I want to bring, must work until ten. Would it be alright to come that late?"

"Heavens yes. The party doesn't get going good until about ten. You'll fit right in."

Between rehearsal and her first show, Cindy and Thomas had dinner. As they were talking Thomas said, "I've been invited to a party tonight. I asked the hostess if it would be too late if I, and my associate, came after ten. She said that the party didn't get going good until ten and it would be okay. I want you to go with me."

"Well, we need to be seen together to make people feel comfortable with us as a couple."

"Are we a couple?"

"Whether you know it or not, you're my beau. I want everyone to know that, so the hussies around town will keep their claws off you."

"I didn't think you were the jealous type."

"I wasn't until I met you, then things changed."

Thomas smiled and said, "Tonight everyone in Colorado Springs will know we're a couple. However, the hostess of this party and I are very close. We traveled together. Please don't make a scene."

After the last show, Cindy made a quick change, but she wore a dress that made her look like the best looking woman in the state. It was gold and fit her body like a glove. She looked extremely good in it.

They were there at about ten thirty. A servant opened the door and gasped."

Thomas said, "Dr. Benson and Miss Lillian Gayle to see Mrs. Emory."

The servant led the way through gasping guests. They reached Mrs. Emory and Thomas embraced her, kissed her on the cheek and said, "You look lovely, Gladys. She just beamed.

Cindy had expected Gladys to be her age and glamorous. She thought, *"That Thomas is the limit, I was worried he had another girl."*

Gladys turned and saw Cindy about the time Thomas said, "Mrs. Emory, Lillian Gayle."

Gladys was stunned, but she recovered quickly and said, "I had no idea Thomas moved in such large circles. You are so welcome, Miss Gayle. Gladys then introduced her husband who was now tongue tied."

Everyone wanted to meet Cindy and shake her hand.

While she was doing that Gladys said, "Thomas you rogue, why didn't you tell me you were bringing Miss Gayle?"

"I wanted to surprise you Gladys."

"Thank you for using my first name like we were old friend, then hugging and kissing me, made my day. Everyone of my friends will now want to know how we became so close. It may make Calvin here a little more interested."

Calvin smiled and said, "I would like to get to know Miss Gayle as well as you know Thomas."

Gladys laughed and said, "Good luck."

Cindy addressed the crowd and said, "I had no idea that Doctor Benson was taking me to a party of Colorado Springs' elite society. What a thrill for me. I sing in many cities, but this is the most elegant party I've been to. It's really nice."

"Everyone clapped then the mayor said, "I know it's rude of me to ask, but would you sing just one song for us? We're all fans of yours and it would mean so much."

She sang a love song that a pianist knew. It had words that a woman would tell her lover. Her eyes never left Thomas' eyes during the song. He was nearly embarrassed as the words were so poignant and obviously meant for him.

The party was grand but Thomas and Cindy left just an hour later. As they traveled Thomas said, "You almost embarrassed me with that song, Cindy."

She said, "I meant every word I said. I have never felt this way."

"Are you suggesting marriage?"

"Not yet, we need time to let this settle."

"I think you're right. If we are apart awhile, I think we will have a better understanding of our relationship."

Nothing was said for awhile then Thomas said, "I'm thinking of building a house. Colorado Springs seems to be a nice place to live. Not too big, but big enough to furnish the things that make living easy."

"Yes, if you have the money."

"We have not talked about money, Cindy. Do you have a financial goal."

"I just have savings and it's not enough to retire on. I suppose I'll sing as long as I'm making money at it. I love to perform. I guess it gets in your blood."

"I have a legacy left by my father who was a successful banker. It's enough that I don't have to work, but I know I should."

"Why did you quit being a doctor?"

"I don't know if I ever quit. I just wanted to be away from where I was. I loved the work and was good at it. I may return to it, but not right away. I've thought about buying a house on a piece of land. Houses are generally a good investment."

"Are you going to make Colorado Springs your home?"

"For now, I'll see how it goes. It's centrally located for your work, so I'll see you ever so often."

Thomas left her at the door of the hotel and drove away to the livery stable.

CHAPTER 20

BUILDING

They talked a lot about their relationship. They decided not to sleep together unless they decided to marry. Actually it was Thomas who did the deciding. If he gave her the word, she would have been in bed with him that night.

He was attracted to her, but didn't know if it were true love, or mostly lust. She had a body that would attract any man. She also had a beautiful face and voice. She sang to sold out crowds every night and made a good salary. Her manager, Lon Perry, was her voice coach, also, and he knew his business. His show was not just Lillian, but she was the main attraction. They played from Cheyenne to Albuquerque. There was a lot of competition in the East, but in the West, there were many more woman-starved men who would pay a great price to see a woman perform who was as lovely as Lillian.

Lon had other acts performing, but mostly women. He had them wear as few clothes as the law would allow. They did risqué things while performing, that would drive the men crazy. The acts were also funny. Lon wrote and directed all the acts.

The troupe was making a lot of money. Lon was generous and paid his troupe well. Cindy left with the troupe for Pueblo on Monday.

Thomas went over to Britton's shop quite often during the design phase. They settled on a price of five thousand dollars plus money for changes. Bob was a master at his craft. He showed Thomas all the latest appliances he planned for the house. The house had a basement, and he put in a furnace with steam heat. He sealed each door and put in new windows that were thicker than ordinary windows. He said, "The house will be warm at forty below zero. He was only able to put in fireplaces in three bedrooms, but Thomas' room had one.

Thomas met Bob's brother Bill. He was invited over to a house that Bill was building and Thomas could see that these boys knew their craft. Bill promised to get started on his place as soon as Bob gave him the plans.

As Thomas was walking from the hotel to the livery stable, one of the three men who had accosted Tom Watson and him on the way to Canon City spotted him. He quickly hid himself and Thomas didn't see him.

The boy's name was Walter Mize. He was living with Bobby Lynn's mother. He had told her of the tragedy, and she took compassion on him and his bother Lee. They had lived with her about a month when Bobby Lynn's brother, Billy Joe retuned from California.

Billy Joe heard the story, and immediately wanted to find the man who killed Bobby Lynn. However, Walter convinced him that the men were headed west to parts unknown and that it may be impossible to find them.

Now that he had seen Thomas coming from the hotel, he raced home to bring the news. Billy Joe wanted to know where he had seen the man.

Walter was out of breath when he reached home, but was able to say, "I just saw the man who killed Bobby Lynn. I think he lives at the hotel. If we are out in front of the hotel in the morning, we'll see him come out. Billy Joe agreed to that, as he wanted to check his pistol and be dressed properly, so he could intimidate Bobby Lynn's killer.

Billy Joe had run with some outlaws in Arizona and thought he was as tough as they come. He had practiced a fast draw, and thought he was the best. He had killed two men facing him. Both times he had made them sweat, and then out drew them.

The next morning Thomas was dressing to do some work out at his place. He had seen a rattle snake the day before, but was not wearing his side arm. He strapped it on, and tied it down.

As he left the hotel for the livery stable he saw a man across the street standing with the two who had accosted he and Tom Watson.

He immediately sensed trouble. That old feeling he had during the war came crawling over him. He changed directions, and walked directly toward them. This surprised

Billy Joe. This man seemed to recognize him, and to his knowledge he had never seen him. The man had a look on his face that made him know he could not be intimidated.

When Thomas got to within sixty feet of the three men, he stopped and said, "If you've come for trouble, I'm your man. But just know if you reach for that gun, I'm going to kill you and those two boys with you. If you want to stay alive, just turn and go."

Billy Joe said, "Are you the man who gunned down Bobby Lynn?"

"Yes, I'm the one. I warned him just like I'm warning you. I've had to kill several men who thought they were tough. Those kind never live to see their thirtieth birthday. So if you're planning on living beyond today, you might think of that.

"I killed Bobby Lynn, but it was he who drew first. Just ask that trash with you."

"Is that true, Walter?"

Walter nodded then said, "I'm not in this, Mister. Billy Joe, here, wanted to know who killed his bother, and I'm just here to show him."

Billy Joe turned and said, "Walter, you were always a coward, I think I might just kill you after I finish with Bobby Lynn's killer."

Thomas just stood there ready to draw. The longer Billy Joe stood there, the less he wanted to confront Thomas. He remembered that Bobby Lynn was fairly fast with a gun, maybe as fast he was. He finally said, "Another time."

In a loud voice Thomas said, "No! We're going to settle this now! You either draw or leave town. If I see you or that trash with you again, I'll gun you down where you stand."

Billy Joe and the Mize brothers left and went home. Billy Joe said, "Ma, we have to pullout. We just got an opportunity and don't want to pass it up." They were gone an hour later.

Thomas left for the livery stable, but now had a bad feeling toward Colorado Springs. He thought, "*This may be just a anomaly that may never come up again. But, it's still the uncivilized West where men like Bobby Lynn lived. I wonder how many Bobby Lynn's there are in and about Colorado Springs. Probably not many, but still there are some. I hate that feeling that comes over me when gun trouble comes. Will I ever lose it? Probably not, that's probably what keeps me alive.*"

He arrived at the building site, and it was busy. They were at the barn first as it was the easiest. One of the crew was a Mexican about forty. He was wiping his brow, when Thomas walked up with his canteen and offered the man a drink.

The man smiled and said, "Thank you, Senor.

Thomas asked, "Do you speak English?"

"Si, but not so good."

"Sounds pretty good to me. What's your name?

"Manuel Gomez."

"Are you married, Manuel?"

"Si. We had two daughters, but they have married and are gone."

Thomas always spoke to him when he was at the worksite. He noticed that Manuel was just a laborer and did little carpentry work.

He talked to Bill Britton about Manuel. Bill said, "Yeah, I've had Manuel a couple of years now. I pay him a dollar a day and he works hard."

The next time Thomas had a chance to talk to Manuel he asked, "Have you ever done any farm work, Manuel?"

Manuel smiled and said, "Si. I was raised on a farm. I was fifteen when my father died. We were just sharecroppers, so they asked us to leave. We came north, as my mother had a cousin in Colorado who said there was work. I came to Pueblo where I met my wife. We were married and I have had work here and there until I was hired by Senior Britton.

"Do you rent or own a home."

"We rent a small house. I just never seem to be able to save, as something always comes up."

"Do you ever do any banking?"

"No, but my wife Kari, does. She worked for a woman who had her do her banking, as she could not leave the house."

"I was thinking, after the house is built, I would like to employ you and Kari. You would live in the house and do the farming that is necessary. I'm also going to run a few head of cattle. You would be paid fifty dollars a month. Kari must keep the house and cook. You would occupy a bedroom on the ground floor. I will go over the running of the place with you and Kari and you would help make the decisions just like an owner. Kari would be our banker and pay the bills. Discuss this with Kari tonight and give me your answer tomorrow.

Manuel was stunned. This house was a mansion to him. Steam heat, indoor plumbing, a marvelous kitchen and their own bathroom. Kari would be ecstatic.

The next day Kari came with Manuel to work. They had a buggy pulled by an old horse. As they were driving up, Thomas thought, *"That's where they get the saying 'A one horse town.'"*

Thomas was introduced to Kari and Thomas showed her the house and where they would be living. Their bedroom was large enough for a sitting room and had it's own bath. There were two doors. One opened into the great room and the other to the kitchen. Kari was thrilled with all the modern appliances and a sink with hot and cold water to it. Thomas showed her the kerosene stove that had an oven. There was also a pantry.

Thomas saw Cindy now and again, but for just short periods of time. Their romance did not flourish, but it was nice when they were together.

A year had passed and the house was finished except for the painting. As Kari walked through the house, Thomas watched her face. She wore a smile and Thomas thought, *"These people will appreciate the place."*

Thomas talked to Bill and said, "I want to hire Manuel and his wife to run this place. I travel a lot and I want someone I trust to tend the place."

"Manuel is a good worker, but I can hire nearly anyone to do his job. I'm happy for Manuel and Kari. Are you going to pay them?"

"Yes, fifty a month. They have a lot of responsibility. Bill laughed and said, "If they don't except the job, maybe Carla and me will apply," and they both laughed."

Thus, life living with the Gomez family started. They sat and planned all the live stock and crops. Kari went over what he liked to eat.

Thomas was on the second floor. He had a balcony that he liked to sit on. He could see the town from there. He liked to have a drink before he went to bed and study the town lighting. Colorado Springs now had gas lit street lights.

Kari went over the menu with Thomas. He said, "I'll eat anything you cook, Kari. I'm well to do, so spend like everything you see in the store is free. Fill the cupboards with only fine dishes and pots and pans. Buy everything you ever wanted. I'm hoping to have ice delivered, so we can utilize that new icebox Bob bought us. I want you to live like you always wanted. I will go by the stores where you want to shop, and start a charge account. You will have to write checks and pay them each month. Your name and Manuel's name will be on the checking account, so Manuel can buy feed and the likes when he needs to. I want you to run this ranch or farm, like you own it. Make good decisions and talk everything over together.

"I'm going to put five thousand dollars in the checking account. Once every year I will go over everything with you, but until then, you're on your own."

They were both in awe. As it was summer, all the windows were open. Thomas could hear them talking half the night, and he smiled.

Thomas showed Cindy the house. One of the bedrooms was converted into a den for Thomas. He had soft chairs a desk and bookcases on the walls. He also had paintings he liked.

Cindy said, "This is a mansion, Thomas. Did you build this for me?"

"Maybe, if things work out with us. Right now you're too busy."

Kari had an office next to the kitchen. She had a desk and

several soft chairs. Thomas had purchased books in Spanish and had put them in a bookcase that covered one wall. She kept meticulous books. The meals she served were different, but Thomas really liked them. Each meal when Manuel prayed, he never prayed without thanking the Lord for their good fortune and Senor Benson.

Thomas went to town each day as he rarely helped around the farm accept when Manuel needed him. He had told Manuel to be sure and ask him to help when it was necessary. So, Manuel was not reluctant to call on Thomas as Manuel put the farm first.

They ran about thirty head of cattle that more than paid the expenses of the farm.

When Cindy was going to be in town, Thomas always stayed in the hotel, now, for her convenience. She was in town, now. They were having dinner and she said, "Lon has been offered a lucrative contract to play in Paris. What do you think of that?"

"Is he going to accept it?"

"He told me he would only take the contract if I went, as that was in the contract."

"Do you want to go?"

"Yes, Thomas. Please go with us. It's a chance of a lifetime."

Thomas could tell she really wanted to go badly, so he said, "Yes, I would like to go." She clutched his hand and said, "Thank you."

They traveled to New York City separately as Thomas wanted to visit some of his friends there. He went to the Dowd's house and could see his parents house was boarded up.

Barney and Betty were thrilled upon seeing him. They

had read the paper about the ship collision and his name was listed with the others as lost. Barney said, "After reading your name as lost, I told Betty we would do nothing about your estate for five years. I don't know why, but I had a feeling you were still alive. Betty told me I was doing the right thing. She also wanted me to wait. We are so glad to see you. Where have you been?"

"I went to Colorado. After losing an associate of mine, I just wanted to live in solitude awhile. I had enough cash and a bank in Denver where I had deposited some money, so I never needed anything. I'm sorry I didn't notify you, but I just couldn't. I didn't want anyone to know. Certainly not my colleagues in Dallas. I see father's home is boarded up."

Dowd said, "I just didn't have the heart to sell it, Thomas. I kept it for you. Betty and I always hoped you would move back here."

"Well, just keep it boarded up for now. Who knows I may want to live in it someday. I'm going to Paris for a few weeks and when I get back I will introduce you a to a woman I'm interested in. That was kind of you to keep the old place. I am very grateful."

CHAPTER 21

TRAVELING

They sailed on the same ship with adjoining cabins. Thomas was having a drink with Lon. Lon said, "When are you going to marry Cindy? I need to know, because it effects the troupe in a big way."

Thomas smiled and said, "I bet when you make love to your wife, you give her a time limit, as not to interfere with business."

Lon laughed and said, "Business is business, Thomas. I have to plan."

"I wish I could give you that answer, Lon, but it will be up to Cindy. I won't chase her around the world watching her perform. When she's ready to quit, then probably then."

"Lon smiled and said, "I'll have to ask her. Things have to be planned."

That night they were having a drink and Thomas asked, "If you are going to be my wife, then you'll have to quit this business. I'm going home when you leave Paris. I'm going to live in my house in Colorado Springs.

"I'll give you a year and if you haven't come, then, I will know you chose your career over me. That's okay. I understand your desire to perform. Just know that you have a year, as I need to get on with my life, and it is surely not following you around."

"Is that an ultimatum?"

"In away, yes."

"I don't like anyone telling me what I must do."

"Well, I guess you just don't love me enough, or I don't love you enough. Let's part friends. Just know this is permanent. I need to get on with my life."

"You said I had a year."

"I don't think you can quit, Cindy. It's in your blood. It's okay, but know that you made the choice."

"She didn't say anything, just looked into her glass."

Thomas left the next morning early, without saying goodbye to anyone.

He was only able to catch a ship going to London. He didn't care, he just knew he had to get out of Paris and away from Cindy. He was hurt deeply, but knew he had made the right choice.

In London he was able to book passage on an ocean liner. He was given a suite on the main deck and ate at the captain's table. He met a few people and talked of current events, but made no friendships.

In New York, he went by to see the Dowd family. Thomas

said, "I want to be go to Colorado and explore that country for awhile. I'm not ready t go back to my work in Dallas, yet."

They both understood and said they would not tell anyone. Thomas left the next day. He took the train to Cheyenne. He enjoyed the solitude. He had a Pullman and the dining was excellent.

When he reached Cheyenne he talked to a stage driver. The driver said, "The army put an end to the Sioux in this area. They have a temporary fort about thirty miles south of here. I guess the Indians went to a place where there were no soldiers. Farming has even started."

Thomas didn't buy a rifle, but he did by a scabbard and pistol. He bought a new western hat and wore levis and a vest. He did wear his suit coat over the vest. It was spring and was warming up. He wanted to see how the grass was on his new place.

They had no trouble. There were only four passengers, so they weren't crowded. All were men. They reached Denver in two and a half days. He went directly to a hotel and changed cloths. He still wore his pistol, but it was covered by his suit coat.

He thought of Connie, but decided to not call on her. He needed solitude, not companionship at this point. He had her address and wrote her a postcard telling her his new address.

He checked the stage to Colorado Springs, and it left at seven the next morning, and would arrive two days later. The first night was spent at a village called Castle Rock. It was located about halfway between Denver and Colorado Springs. It had a decent hotel and a dining room. He washed up and put on clean clothes, then went downstairs to the dinning room. It was after eight when he sat down to eat. His steak was tough, but he didn't complain as the gravy for the potatoes was excellent.

As he was finishing his meal he saw a fight breakout at the bar. He left out the front door to avoid the fight and ran into the sheriff who was running to the door. The collision caused the sheriff to be knocked down as Thomas was much the bigger man. He tried to help the sheriff up, but the sheriff was mad and brushed his hand away and got up by himself.

The sheriff said, "You're under arrest."

"For what, you ran into me."

"You probably caused the fight I was investigating."

"I was not involved in that altercation, I was eating my dinner as the waiter can verify."

The sheriff then pushed pass him going in to the room. The fight had intensified and the two men had drawn their guns. One shot the other in the shoulder causing his shot to go awry and hit the sheriff in the leg.

The door was open so Thomas saw the whole thing. The man who was shot, dropped to the floor and the other man went to him and shot him in the head. He wheeled around toward the sheriff.

The sheriff by this time, was being helped by Thomas, so when the gunman leveled his pistol on the sheriff, Thomas swiftly pulled the sheriff's gun and shot him through the heart. He dropped dead immediately.

The sheriff by this time was seething mad, at being shot. After leaning on the bar he said, "Give me my gun. I'm arresting you for murder."

The bartender, a local doctor and a banker were at the bar and had witnessed the ordeal. Thomas said, "Just ask any of these men, I was acting in self and your defense. The man pointed a gun at us, and you were in front of me and would have been shot had not I taken action."

The doctor was now looking at the sheriff's leg and said, "He's right, Charlie. You would probably be dead had this stranger not helped you by shooting that gunman."

The sheriff still didn't like it. He wanted to blame someone and the only one alive was Thomas. He said, "I don't know who he is or why he interfered with the law."

Thomas said, "I didn't interfere with anyone. I'm just passing through, and don't know anyone in this town besides the other passengers on the stage to Denver."

Thomas recognized one of the men who was on his stage and said, "That man there, can verify I'm a passenger on the stage to Denver."

The man Thomas had pointed to, nodded his head and said, "He's a passenger on the stage to Denver."

The sheriff said, "What's your business?"

Thomas was now irritated and said, "My own business, Sheriff."

"Smart guy are you? I'm placing you under arrest."

"On what charge, Sheriff?"

"The sheriff hemmed and hawed a second or two and said, "For vagrancy."

Thomas pulled out his wallet and showed the sheriff some money. The sheriff said, "How do I know how you came by that money, you probably robbed someone."

"What proof do you have of that?"

Finally he said, "Go to hell. You had better be on that stage tomorrow morning."

"Or you'll what?"

"I'll shoot you down in the street."

"I'll be wearing my gun, Sheriff." He turned to the people at the bar and said, "Let it be known that the sheriff has threatened my life and I have the right to defend myself."

The sheriff was startled then and looked at Thomas more carefully. Thomas had the stone face he had worn in battle. It was a frozen stare at the sheriff saw. He thought, *"That man plans to kill me if I brace him."*

The doctor then said, "You're not going to shoot anyone for a few days, Charlie. I need to get that bullet out of your leg."

A man helped the sheriff walk to the doctors. After he was gone, Thomas turned to the bartender and said, "How did he ever become sheriff?"

"No one else would take the job. We have a rough element here as you just witnessed. Had you not helped him, we would be looking for the forth sheriff this year. None of them were killed, they simple quit when they were confronted. There are men out of work, and they're angry and lawless. Then there's the miners. They don't believe in any law. I don't see Charlie living out the year with his attitude. He's irrational at times as you just witnessed."

Thomas left on the stage the next morning. As he traveled he thought, *"I wonder why things happen to me. First their was the war, then Junior and his father, then the problem with Bobby Lynn and his brother, then the Indians. I seem to attract trouble as well as women.*

"Lesley was the only woman I sought. But even then, she did

most of the pursuing. Then there was Mary. I would have never pursued her. Then Cindy. I would have bet that she would have quit her singing and married me, but she loved her career more than me. Then there was Connie. I was smart to leave her alone. However, I liked her. What's to become of me. Here I'm going to live in a house, and really have nothing to do. Where am I going? I know I don't want to go to Dallas right now, but what? I'm a stranger to myself."

Thomas didn't realize it but a man was talking to him. He then realized it and said, "I'm sorry, I was deep in thought and didn't realize you were talking to me."

The man said, "Did you ever know why that sheriff was so mad at you? All you did was save his life."

"I ran into him when I was leaving. I'm so much bigger that he caught the worse of the collision. However, He must have had a bee stinging him before we collided. He's just a small man with a chip on his shoulder."

"Yeah, it's called the small-man complex. Some small men have to try to prove themselves with larger men because they are small. No one cares but them, but they can't get over it."

The conversation ended and Thomas went back to his self-analyses. *"What did he want to do in life. Would he ever have a wife that loved him like Lesley and Mary?"*

CHAPTER 22

THE RANCH WOMEN

Thomas had left his buggy and horse with the livery. He had to pay a large fee, but collected them and drove to his ranch. It was nice to look at from afar. It sat on a slight rise above all the trees and structures that surrounded it. Bob Britton was so skilled that it looked like a mansion. He had frilled up the barn to match the house in elegance.

He pulled up in front of the house that had a brick circular driveway. Manual was in for lunch and both he and Kari came outside and greeted him.

Kari said, "You're just in time for lunch."

They went in and had a fine lunch. As Kari served coffee they both wanted to tell him what had occurred while he was gone.

Kari then said, "A letter came that they carried out to the

house. It was a letter from Mrs. Connie Sims. She inquired if you lived in Colorado Springs. I took the liberty of answering it and told her you lived here and that I was your maid. I told her you were in Paris, France at the time, but would return.

"We received another letter asking for me to inform her when you returned. Did I do right?"

"You did splendid, Kari."

"I have another request, Senior Benson? Our daughter lost her husband in an accident. She has no place to go, could she come here if we pay you."

"You don't have to pay. I think of you as family, so she is family. Tell her we are looking forward to having her."

Kari said, "You are the kindest man I ever knew. You will love Darlena, she is always happy. Manual said when she left us to get married, that the house would never be as bright again. But, here she is returning to fill your house with laughter and sunshine."

Darlena arrived two weeks later. In the meantime Thomas wrote Connie. He asked if she wanted to visit him. She wrote back that she would like to come and gave the date of two weeks later.

Darlena was everything Kari and Manual had said, "She was not only a happy person but was outstandingly beautiful. She tearfully told how her husband was loading a wagon when another wagon went out of control, and wedged him between the two wagons. He was killed instantly. His family was poor and lived in a one room hovel, but made room for her, anyway.

Darlena was amazed at the house and particularly that she had her own room and bathroom. She was put on the first floor. She volunteered for every chore to the point that Thomas said, "Darlena, you don't have to earn your keep here. We like that you are so helpful, but your parents are a family to me and will live their lives here. That means you can live here forever."

She spontaneously came into his arms and hugged him. Thomas was surprised that he liked the hug so much, but then she was very beautiful. She was all her parents had said about her. She brought sunshine into the home. Thomas could tell how much she meant to Manual and Kari.

Thomas briefed Manual, Kari and Darlena about Connie and how he came to know her. The only one who was not so warm to her visiting was Darlena, as by this time she had formed a fondness for Thomas. However, she put on a happy face like she was anxious to meet Connie.

The day Connie was to arrive, Thomas was there with his buggy. She got off the stage and there stood a smiling Thomas. She came to him and gave him a hug.

She said, "I'm glad to see you Thomas. How long has it been?"

"Nearly two years, now. I thought you would be married again and have a child."

"No, I'm the same girl you left in Denver. Do you have room for me in your house, or should I get a hotel room?"

"I think we can make room for you. I have three other people who live with me. Manual and Kari Gomez are the caretakers, and their daughter recently came to stay with us, as her husband was killed in an accident. We are a family, now."

Connie was surprised that Thomas would count a

Mexican family who worked for him as a family. Her father and mother were both bigoted toward Mexicans and some of it had rubbed off on Connie. She was also hoping to have Thomas alone.

As they traveled Connie said, "I hate to burden you with my troubles, but I feel I have to. My father has become an alcoholic as has my mother. I cannot live with them anymore. I have a sister and brother, but they are in no position to help me.

"I will find a job and try to get on my own as quickly as I can, so not to be a burden on you."

"You did the right thing, Connie. No one should live around abuse if they can help it. I have a large house and you will be no burden at all. We will talk about you working later. I think you will enjoy living with us, and I certainly welcome you."

"Why were you in Paris, Thomas?"

"My girl fiend is a singer and actor. Her troupe was offered a contract to play in Paris and took it. I went over to see that she was okay. You may have heard of her. Her name Is Lillian Gayle."

"My, you have moved up in the world. From being stuck with a girl with no knowledge of how to take care of herself, and having to defend her from Indians to an international celebrity. I've seen pictures of her. How did you meet her?"

Thomas explained about how he met her and how they became enamored with one another until their parting."

"Will you ever get back together?"

"I gave her a year, before I completely closed the books on her."

"This made her angry, so I just left with no goodbyes. So, I really don't know."

From a distance Connie could see the mansion Bob Britton had created. She said, "My lord, is that your house?"

Thomas smiled and said, "A master builder designed the renovation of an old home and made it into a mansion."

"How were you able to pay for such a thing?"

"I was left a legacy and decided I would like to spend part of it on the house as I like to live well."

"Live well! You live like a king!"

They pulled up around the circular driveway and Manual, Kari and Darlena were out to greet Connie.

Manual said, "You are filling up the house with beautiful women, Senor Benson."

Connie spotted Darlena immediately as a rival as she could see her beauty.

Manual had taken her bag and she was led to her room upstairs. She was amazed at the size of her bedroom and particularly with her own bathroom. She had never been in a home of this size and elegance.

Connie put her clothes up then returned downstairs. Everyone was waiting for her and she was handed a glass of fruit punch with rum it. Thomas said, "That drink has rum in it, so if you would prefer one without alcohol, just say so."

Connie said, "No, I would like to try it. I just don't want to end up like my parents."

They sat in the parlor on splendid chairs and coaches. There were nice rugs covering the hardwood. Her eyes surveyed the walls that had several paintings and two tapestries that accented the room.

She said, "You people are rich. I've never been to such a luxurious place. My, I am overwhelmed."

Kari said, "We all were too, Mrs. Sims."

"Please call me Connie. I'm just plain Connie."

"Darlena said, "You are anything but plain, Connie. You are a beautiful woman who fits this mansion."

"You all are so kind. I left Denver because I cannot live there anymore. I will seek a job and try to be on my own as soon as I can."

Darlena was thinking, *"That can't be too soon as far as I'm concerned."*

Connie said, "I'm not above cleaning the house, Kari. Just assign me work like I was a maid."

"We'll get into that soon enough, Connie, for now we just want to enjoy you," Thomas said.

Connie did fit in and Darlena and her became friends. They both confessed that they were enamored with Thomas, but that he would do nothing until a year passed. Both said, "He'd never take either of us over Lillian Gayle."

Thomas convinced Connie that she didn't need to have a job. He paid both Darlena and Connie twenty dollars a month. He said, "You both earn it. You keep this place spotless, do the laundry and help in many ways. This house needs both of you as it is a job cleaning a place this large."

Thomas bought a piano when he found that Connie played. It was a grand piano that was the finest. It fit like it was made to be in the great room. They would stand around the piano and sing some nights. Connie was an accomplished musician as her father had taught her to play when she was young.

They sang Spanish songs as well as American tunes. They also played cards and other games. It was a happy house and *Thomas thought, "This is what I always wanted, a big happy family. If Cindy does show up, I'm sure she would destroy it."*

Three months later, Darlena found she was pregnant. She was as surprised as all of them. She said, "I am so glad. I have something from Gerome."

Connie said, "Thomas and I will join your father and mother, Darlena, in being a parent."

Darlena became serious then and said, "We can't dote on him. We must make sure he grows up like Thomas."

Thomas said, "What if it is a girl?"

"Then she will grow up like Connie." and everyone laughed.

Connie insisted in doing any of Darlena's work that would cause her stress. Dalena said, "You are now spoiling me. I see raising our child will be very difficult."

* * *

The winter passed and spring was on it's way out as they were having very warm weather. All the doors and windows were open. Kari was taken into town in the buggy by Connie and Manuel was out in the field.

Cindy had come into town and had hired a man to take her to Thomas' house in his buggy. She arrived and no one heard the buggy drive up. She went up to the door and could see Thomas in the living room. He said, "Darlena," which sounded like *darling* to Cindy, "Would you bring me the coffee I left on the kitchen table?"

Cindy could see a beautiful woman, who was large with child, come into the room. She was petrified.

Just then Thomas spotted her at the door and came and said, "Cindy, I didn't hear you drive up. Let me pay the hack for you," and after giving her a small hug went to pay the hack.

Cindy was now in the house and Darlena knew immediately who she was. She was past beautiful, she was gorgeous. She wore an orange gown that must have cost fifty dollars. Her hair was perfect and her figure even better.

"You must be Miss Gayle," Darlena opined. She could see how Cindy stared at her stomach, and being very bright, understood immediately that Cindy thought it was Thomas' child.

Darlena said, "Yes, I'm due any day now. Thomas has even made a room and put in a place for him to deliver my baby. Of course you know how attentive he is."

"Did Thomas tell you about me?"

"Yes, of course. Wouldn't you expect him to?"

"Yes, I guess he would have to, knowing Thomas and his honesty."

About that time Thomas returned with her bags and said, "You didn't give us any warning."

"I can now see I should have," as she looked at Darlena.

It never entered Thomas mind that Cindy would think that the baby Darlena carried was his. He smiled and said, "She's due any day now. Would you care for a cool drink?"

"I think I need a stiff one, make it a double. Scotch if you have it."

It then began to dawn on Thomas that Cindy thought it was his baby.

He laughed inwardly and said, "I have some scotch that I think you'll like. I didn't ever see you drink in the morning, but I guess you were shocked seeing Darlena that large."

Cindy said, "When did you get married?"

Now Thomas was having fun with the situation and said, "Oh, we're not married. You'll see why when the other girls return from town."

Darlena caught on that Thomas was having fun with her and said, "You'll love Connie. She was stranded with Thomas for days, when they were attacked by Indians. You'll really like her. We've all become close."

Thomas handed her the scotch and she downed it in one swallow, and handed him the glass and said, "Please fix me another."

Thomas then thought he had better tell her and said, "Darlena is Manuel's and Kari's daughter. Her husband was killed in an accident, but left Darlena something to remind her of him."

Cindy looked at him and said, "That's just like you Thomas Benson. Play me like a fiddle and have fun doing it."

"I'll have to admit I left you hanging for awhile, but you should know I don't sleep with women I'm not married to."

Cindy looked at Darlena and said, "I can vouch for that. I should have known, but I thought he called you darling when I was at the door, so I just assumed the worst."

Darlena said, "I'm not so sure it would have been the worst."

"I should have known, you love him, too. When Connie get's here, we can form a club."

This made Darlena laugh out loud. She said, "Thomas told us you had a good sense of humor."

"What else did he tell you?"

"About everything he knew. He's quite taken with you."

"Was," as in the past tense?"

"No, now that you're here before the year is out, you're still in the present tense."

"Did he tell you about the mole on my back."

Darlena was quick and said, "No, will you show it to us?"

Cindy looked at Thomas and said, "I can see why you like her, Thomas, not only beautiful, but with a quick wit. I think I like her, too."

About that time the girls came driving up. They yelled, "We need some help with the groceries." Thomas, Darlena and Cindy appeared.

Connie said, "My lord, Kari that is Lillian Gayle!"

The both stood in awe, until Cindy said, "Just call me Cindy as I'm now just one of Thomas' many women," which made them all laugh.

Darlena said, "She's a good sport as when she arrived she thought that I was carrying Thomas' baby, so we had a little fun with her."

Cindy said, "With all these beautiful women, I'm glad I'm still in the running," which made them all laugh. "I now see you why Thomas bought this huge house. Are there anymore coming, Thomas?"

Thomas defused the comment by saying, "Let's get these groceries in the house." They all took several arm loads as Kari had bought groceries for a week.

They had just finished with the groceries, when Manual arrived. He was polite and kept out of the way as all the girls were in the kitchen now, as Kari prepared lunch. Both Connie and Darlena helped set the table in the dining room as the kitchen table was too small for all of them.

After lunch the girls started cleaning the table and Connie said to Cindy, "Why don't you two take a walk. I'm sure you have a lot to talk about." However, she was thinking, *"I would surely like to hear their conversation."*

Cindy said, "Thanks Connie."

They left toward a landscaped garden at the rear of the house. Under a giant elm tree there was a bench. They sat there and Thomas asked, "Well, have you made up your mind."

"Yes, I quit Lon and told him I wanted marriage rather than a career. After you left, singing became a chore to me. When I was singing, the songs became only about you. I love you completely, Thomas. I can only be happy if you are with me. If you'll have me, I want to be your wife and give you children."

"Then it's settled. We'll get married next Saturday. You will become part of our family. As you can see, I love them all, but I am in love with only you."

They kissed and went back into the house. They were all in the parlor now and Thomas said, "I would like you to meet the future Mrs. Thomas Benson. We will be married Saturday."

Kari said, "Couldn't you give us a little more time. I'm sure Gladys Emory would like to throw you a reception."

Thomas turned to Cindy and said, "What do you say, Cindy?"

Cindy said, "Kari you plan it and take all the time you want. I'll need time to get a wedding dress."

Just at that time Darlena said, "It's time Thomas," and began heading for the room they had prepared. Kari turned to boil water and Connie caught Darlena's arm to helped her.

Cindy said, "That's my Thomas. The minute he's engaged, he takes one of his women and delivers her baby."

THE END

Printed in the United States
By Bookmasters